HELL'S
PLAYGROUND

JIL PLUMMER

Andrew Benzie Books
Walnut Creek, California

Published by Andrew Benzie Books
www.andrewbenziebooks.com

*This work is a fictionalized story based on the experiences of
John Davison in the Vietnam War. In order to maintain anonymity,
in some instances names of individuals have been changed.*

Printed in the United States of America

First Edition: September 2018

10 9 8 7 6 5 4 3 2 1

ISBN 978-1-941713-81-5

www.jilplummer.com

Cover and book design by Andrew Benzie

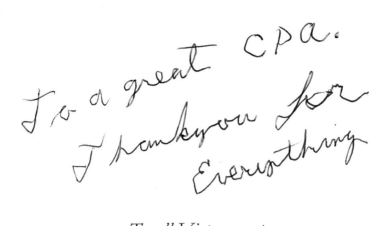

To a great CPA.
Thank you for Everything

To all Vietnam veterans

Sincerely

John R Davison

John and friend, road to Saigon, 1968

THEY DIDN'T KNOW HOW

They say to get your education. They say to get it now.
They say to study very hard, even if you don't know how.
But I don't want my education. I don't want it now,
Because I have to fight,
And fight I don't know how.
I arrived in Vietnam on an August day.
Saw the battle raging, heard the people pray.
The lieutenant screamed "Fire!" And we fired our guns.
I felt the heat of hell pressing on my lungs.
Then I felt a blinding pain shoot fast through my head.
I lay there on the hot, green grass—bloody and almost dead.
My friend lay there next to me and whispered as he died,
"Keep on fighting strong, my friend, for freedom's on our side."
But freedom's killing many of those people whom I love.
It twists them and it thrusts them into the skies above.
But I must admit it would surely be a shame
To have to fight on US soil and lose all that I claim.
Yes we must fight until the battle's won.
To shoot, kill and destroy, these things must be done.
So through the smoke and thunder I will make my way
While praying for a peaceful world for us to have some day.

A poem from the heart by John Robert Davison

PROLOGUE

My name is John Davison and this is my own story of what I experienced in the Vietnam war during one of the worst prison riots in military history.

I really believed once I got home to the USA I would have it made. Nothing could be further from the truth; I came home to a world of indifference and complete lack of compassion for Vietnam veterans.

To be quite frank I was so glad to be alive I didn't give a damn what anybody thought of me.

I've experienced bouts of severe depression ever since the war and it has cost me dearly.

Please read this book with a clear head and a kind heart.

Sincerely,
John Davison

CHAPTER ONE
Hell's Playground

Something moved behind him. Spec5 John Davison reached for the forty-five that should be tucked under his left armpit. Sweat of Vietnam soaked his shirt but a voice in his head shouted, "No!" Just in time he clasped his hands behind his back to keep them still and returned himself back to the room in which he was about to be interviewed for his first job since deployment.

Did a soldier ever get over it? Go back to being the innocent, fun loving student? John had chosen to study Law Enforcement at the local college, then go on to Northern Arizona University. He knew he was expected to eventually follow in his father's footsteps and become a joke telling super salesman just like him, but he needed to get away from home and the stress of an alcoholic mother. Maybe he liked law enforcement because he had been bullied as a child until his dad initiated boxing lessons which gave him the power to stand up for himself and "be a man." As a cop he could help people in trouble; he would really like a chance to do that. Maybe focus on kids like those around him who were getting into drugs and stealing cars; ending up in jail. Once he'd gone on a tour of juvenile hall and thought of being shut up in one of those small cells was so claustrophobic he'd had nightmares for weeks afterward. As a cop maybe he could save kids from that too common fate.

Home on break from college John listened to Elvis Presley and cruised his semi-rural neighborhood in his beloved pea green Chevy, looking good to the girls he was too shy to ask out. He was popular at parties for his guitar playing and singing the often humorous songs he made up; making people laugh was like alcohol to him although he was well supplied with that too.

Mornings John often spent hiking the East bay hills with his Irish Setter, Shannon, pausing to watch the sun rise from behind Mount Diablo and then turning to look at the sparkling sea which stretched out to forever beyond the Golden Gate. He had an itch to do something, go somewhere big. Vietnam was all over the news but he hadn't paid a lot of attention and didn't know what to think of the war there. Everyone talked about it. Some 'for', some more violently 'against.'

All young men felt the draft breathing down their necks and some planned on running up to Canada to escape it. John figured if his number was drawn he'd do his duty and go. No one was going to call him a coward. If President Johnson said the war was necessary it must be so. He had no doubts about his president. For him his country's leader could do no wrong. What the hell, he'd always dreamed of travelling hadn't he? Maybe this would be his chance. It might even be fun!

CHAPTER TWO

The letter came thirty days after graduation. Mother wept and poured another glass of gin.

It seemed no time until it was the designated morning of his departure and his mother was hugging him a tearful goodbye. Even his sister was wet eyed.

"Keep the battery alive in my car and above all look after Shannon," were John's last words to her as he ruffled his dog's ears.

"Come on, Son, gotta get moving," said Dad, clearing his throat.

John got into his dad's Ford after first placing his cased guitar carefully on the back seat. "Jeez, you'd think I was going off to war or something. Hell, it's only boot camp. War'll be over before I'm ready, the president says so." He said this to placate his dad but inside his heart was pumping fast with the excitement of hopefully being in the thick of it. A hero like Gregory Peck in 'Guns of the Navaronne'.

His dad's Adam's apple bobbed up and down a moment but he said nothing.

John looked out the window watching struts of the Bay bridge flash past and seeing sun strike the distant SF Ferry building. Shouldn't he be sad to leave home instead of just excited at starting off on an adventure? Sure, some guys died but according to President Johnson not that many. But, was this maybe, the last time he'd see these familiar sights? He shook off morbid thoughts and tried to imagine Fort Lewis. He'd never been to the state of Washington. But first would be a few days in an Oakland barracks. He hadn't told anyone that. It seemed kind of anticlimactic after all his good byes and stuff.

"Here we are," said his dad, pulling into a parking place outside the San Francisco bus station.

The sidewalk was a sea of young men of all shapes and sizes, but seeming mostly black and tough looking with scars and tattoos and hard, bloodshot eyes. What white guys there were had congregated in one area and some of them, John noticed, had hair even longer than his. One thing every man had in common was the knapsack slung over his shoulder. John's stomach churned and he wondered how he'd been so blasé about this whole thing. He'd convinced himself this was nothing but a great adventure, an escape from home to be a patriot and a hero, but suddenly there it was on the newspaper rack in front of him—a front page full of the latest offensive in Vietnam. It was called Tet.

His dad was beside him saying something about buying a bunch of hot dogs. "God knows when you boys'll get a chance to eat. Be right back…"

"No Dad wait!" but he was gone, running across the street toward a sign advertising "Kelly's Dogs."

A whistle blew and a red faced man with sergeant stripes on his khaki uniform bellowed for men taking the bus to Fort Lewis, Washington to get on board.

For a moment John considered chasing after his dad, then he was being jostled and shoved toward the waiting Greyhound. Truncated farewells were being shouted back and forth between abruptly torn apart families and John tried to spot his father but couldn't.

He was carried in what felt like a killer riptide toward the bus, pushed up the steps and then into an aisle seat. Frantically John stuffed his belongings into the overhead rack and, gripping the guitar case between his knees, craned to see out the window which his seat partner had opened and now leaned out of, waving and blocking most of the view.

Then there he was! His dad, running, crimson faced, arms filled with bags of hot dogs, surely enough for everyone on the bus. His mouth was open, shouting.

The doors snapped shut and with a roar the bus pulled away. In horror John saw his dad stop and watch after it with a terrible empty look of despair. Dozens of hot dogs fell, scattering over the ground around his feet.

John had never felt so bereft in his life, and he would never forget that sight of his robust father in his weakest moment.

The bus was quiet but for the moan of its engines. The men-boy passengers avoided each other's eyes and locked into their own thoughts.

It felt really anticlimactic to find himself again crossing the bridge only to be deposited in Oakland, a few miles from home and parents who by now thought him far away. Probably in their imaginings he was already under fire in Vietnam. Being a hero, no doubt! Well, they need never know.

The bus entered through a gate guarded by sentries and stopped in front of several camouflaged buildings. The instant the doors opened the shouting of orders began, each one bellowed at the top of an NCO's lungs as the new recruits descended.

The next three days were spent waiting, bored out of his mind, being interviewed for some indefinable purpose and given instructions so full of army terms and insults no one understood them. At first John thought it odd how every recruit seemed closed into himself, not wanting to speak to others; unlike college where students had quickly made friends and shared the adventure of that new life. 'Is it because we have nothing in common except for ignorance of what is to come?'

John, at supper, on the third evening before leaving for 'up North' next morning wondered if maybe his dreams of being a hero for the good ol' USA had cast too much of a rosy glow on this whole venture. "College gave us hope for a bright future. Vietnam may promise no future." Someone back home had said that. He turned those thoughts off and piled more mashed potatoes onto his plate. At least the food was half decent.

CHAPTER THREE

At last they were on the road North. John still wore his jeans and favorite Pendleton shirt which after three days was not feeling like his favorite anymore.

He felt a stir of excitement when the bus crossed the border into Oregon. They were let out at a roadside park to use the restrooms and eat sandwiches distributed by the military driver. From the way his fellow travelers were looking around John realized that many had probably never been outside the inner city before. They actually seemed afraid of this alien natural world. It did not build confidence to think his life might depend on this scraggly bunch of young men. Wouldn't be surprised if they ran at the first sign of action. Some of them reminded him of when he used to caddy at the golf club in Orinda. Often boys from poor neighborhoods in Richmond would wait outside the club gates to heckle and sometimes physically attack him and the other caddies as they left. These outsiders demanded that they should have the jobs not these local rich kids. It had surprised John to have his family thought of as rich. Looking around the bus now he noticed differences and it wasn't just skin color. Before today, meeting one of these guys on the street might just have tempted him to cross over to the other side but now they just looked scared and young.

His thoughts wandered to Vietnam. Jungles. Natives who lived in huts maybe and spoke some weird other language. They'd be happy to see Americans come to their rescue for sure. Yeah, he'd fight for the right, stick it to those commies and then be welcomed home as a hero. He'd be 'somebody' in that little hometown. Maybe they'd even have a parade for him! Yes, he really had a lot to look forward to.

He dozed and watched the passing landscape. Mostly forest now. Kid next to him slept with his mouth open. A mosquito buzzed perilously close and John was tempted to either push the mouth shut or smash the bug. On second thoughts he did neither.

On arrival at Fort Lewis they stepped out into the crisp rain drenched night. John sucked in gulps of fresh air which after the sickly stuffiness of the bus was like water to someone lost in a desert.

They were herded into a mess hall, given a meal, which was delicious only because they had eaten nothing but increasingly soggy sandwiches all day, then they were sent to a barracks to seek out their designated bunks.

His was a lower one for which he was glad as he flopped into it thinking he was too sleepy to have ever made it into the one above.

CHAPTER FOUR

What the hell!? Lights blazed and what sounded to be a garbage can lid clattered past, followed by a sergeant banging metal lids together as he bellowed for them to get their sorry asses out of bed, calling them MFs and things John had never heard of before. He scrambled into his clothes, then went into the large wash room.

"God almighty it's four am," someone muttered.

"Into the Mess, you sons of bitches. Three minutes to chow down and you're outa here. Move it !"

John grabbed his plate of scrambled eggs and stuffed forkful after forkful into his mouth, washing it down with milk 'til he feared he might choke. Still chewing he left the room accompanied by an NCO's voice berating them for being slow; driving them on to the next step which was lining up for fatigues, underwear, socks and boots.

John figured he looked good in his new starched fatigues but there was no full length mirror to see himself in, just faucets which reflected countless warped kaki clad gnomes. No time anyway as he was shouted into a room with a dozen barber chairs where men sat down with a full head of hair and rose a few moments later with a head like the butt of a plucked chicken. Some of the previously long haired dudes left with tears in their eyes. John didn't mind much as he'd never been that focused on his hair. Previously sun bleached and shaggy he imagined he liked the new tough look. That is until he went outside and felt cold rain pattering on his bald dome. Quickly he dragged on the cap he'd been issued and went to stand in line with others of his group.

"Move it, you maggots!"

John already hated the NCO who cut them down with every degrading word; told them to turn left and cursed them for being slow, then "right" calling them morons till every man was so completely flustered he couldn't do anything.

"I'm going to work you gentlemen until you enjoy killing. When you get to Nam you'll be ready to kill anything that moves." He leaned toward them, spittle flying. "You hear me crapheads! You're gonna kill, kill kill 'cause that's why you're here."

John was aware of some of the guys being swept along with the rhetoric but everything within him recoiled. "I sure hope I never have to kill anyone!" It burst out loud and clear.

A voice from the back yelled, "Davison won't shoot. He'll get us all killed!"

He felt the anger toward the NCO being transferred to him but immediately they were sent running on a trail through the woods. John was fairly fit from hiking the hills around home but some of the recruits were gasping for breath by the first quarter mile. "You son of a bitch babies. Move it! One two three four."

John knew about boot camp. He'd been told by a friend's brother who'd been home on leave before shipping out on his first tour of duty. He'd said it was all put on to toughen them up but it was a bitch while it lasted. They had slowed to a walk. Now, as he plodded through the dripping forest, feeling his toes squelch in his boots, John thought of the guy who'd told him that. Hadn't done him much good—he'd never come home.

It was so damn cold. Rain drummed down harder. They'd been marching for what seemed hours. Then suddenly they were back at the barracks and after a few minutes of being made to stand at shivering attention they were dismissed with orders to shower and change into their second pair of fatigues before going to the mess hall.

Hot water just had time to chase the numbness from John's chilled frame before he was shoved out to make room for another shivering miserable recruit. A joke or encouraging word had always been on the tip of John's tongue for friend or stranger and he almost made some flip remark now, but stifled it. This was a different world. He had to be a different man.

He remembered that thought ten minutes later when, on his way to the mess, a voice stopped him short. "Davison!"

John turned reluctantly toward the NCO who had been haranguing them all day.

"Sir?"

"We need more men in charge here and I want you, and others I choose with college educations, to act as temporary NCOs. You'll have stripes and privileges."

"And what would I have to do, Sir?"

"Just what you've seen me do, keep the scum in line. It's a good deal, Davison."

"Not me, Sir, I couldn't do it, Sir. Sorry Sir."

"Got no balls, Davison?"

"Guess not, Sir. Not for that, anyway. Sir."

With a look of disgust the officer left him and John moved on into the chow line.

"He try to make you do tough guy job?"

Surprised, John looked down at the short, stocky man at his elbow. He had a wide grin, high flat cheek bones, slightly squinting eyes and a tan complexion.

"Yeah, turned him down though.'"

"Ah, he'll get men enough. Guys who like to do that stuff. Chew people out."

Both new recruits stacked their plates as full as they'd hold and walked together to a table. For a few minutes they just stuffed food into their mouths. John had never felt so hungry.

"Where do you think I'm from?"

"No idea," mumbled John through a mouth full of meat loaf.

"I'm Eskimo." Dark eyes sparkled as though it was the biggest joke in the world.

John stopped chewing. "You guys still live in igloos?"

"Of course. Build 'em new each Spring."

"They melt?"

"Sure, all that new fangled central heating, y'know!" The man's whole swarthy face crumpled into laughter. "Got cha that time!"

"Sorry, I guess I never met an Eskimo before. Just in kids' books, maybe."

"No problem. Hey, my name's Mann, Ben Mann."

"And mine's John Davison. Good to know you!"

They shook hands, grinned at each other then went back to gulping their food. Suddenly John felt better about this damn camp—he had a friend.

Next day several of the new recruits had removable stripes pinned to their shoulders and trotted around giving orders and insults as though they'd had classes from the real NCOs. John would have been ashamed to be one of them. But Ben just grinned and shrugged. Nothing fazed him.

Things were better now. John had made friends with another soldier also and joking around among the three of them put a better perspective on Boot Camp life. He learned things from them, such as how the act of pouring milk over everything made it easier to swallow more food in the allotted three minutes. Up until now he'd not had a moment when his stomach hadn't ached from hunger. Even better was when Ben took him out behind the kitchen where the empty milk cartons were tossed, many still with a good gulp of milk left in them.

Days folded into each other; all cold to California boys, most wet and every one containing what seemed an endless hike with continual harassment and debasement. John almost enjoyed learning to handle the m16 although his fingers were so numb he could hardly pull the trigger. He was a good shot, probably the best there, so the Sergeant had a hard time criticizing him. Instead he found other ways to dig.

Some men broke under the strain. Rumor had it that one smallish guy went into the chapel in the middle of the night and drove a knife into his heart, bleeding to death right there on the altar steps. John figured the kid was probably on drugs but hoped the suicide wasn't true, although one soldier who had been hassled savagely yesterday was missing from the ranks today.

No one paid much attention to the new guys with the phony stripes who, even though they tried throwing their weight around, did not have the talent to hurt that the three real NCOs had. They were artists at their game of tearing a man down, although John swore he'd never let them get to him.

One morning in the mess they almost did.

"Davison, your boots look like shit. Come up here so I can show the rest of this mangy troop how you disrespect the US army. Move it, Private. Bring your plate of grub."

Bewildered, John walked to the front of the room where the Sergeant waited.

"Turn around. Put the tray on your head. Now eat!"

Porridge, bacon and eggs, toast, jam and coffee slid, spilled and splattered as John tried to do as he was ordered. Every face was turned toward him, laughing at his struggle as the NCO taunted him for the mess he was making. Finally the hot coffee tipped and crashed to the floor.

"Go clean up, you're nothing but a pig. Were you brought up in a sty?"

The laughing continued.

John grabbed the tray from his head and dropped it with what food was left on it onto the nearest table. He headed for the door.

"Private Davison. Don't you know to ask permission to leave and are you too stupid to remember how to address your superior?"

"Yes, Sir, no Sir. May I go sir?" and he bolted back to his locker where he grabbed a towel and pushed it into his face. For the first time since he was a child John Davison wept.

CHAPTER FIVE
Boot Camp Week Three

It was cold and the long marches were painful survival.

Inside the barracks, each room was heated by a potbellied iron stove.

One night John awoke coughing and discovered he could barely see the bunk across the aisle from his. When he turned on his flashlight it was no better. He flung off his blankets and ran to the main light switch only to see black smoke swirling through cracks in the stove's tin chimney. Now other men, coughing and spluttering, ran to the outside door and flung it open, trying to catch their breath.

They stood shivering, hacking and retching until the coals died and they could reenter the now frigid but bearably smoke free room.

They blocked what cracks they could but on following nights preferred smoky warmth to freezing sleeplessness so many men were coming down with upper respiratory infections. John was not sorry when his turn came to be ordered off to the hospital. What bliss it was to lie between clean sheets in a warm, quiet room with no one yelling at him. Antibiotics soon had him back in the line but now the harassment didn't bother him as much and he and Ben both agreed that one of the sergeants probably wouldn't be a half bad guy in real life.

Although each day seemed forever, suddenly the twelve weeks were over. After breakfast all the recruits, dressed today in the civvies they had arrived in, were ordered to collect their packed duffles and line up on the parade ground. John was heading off to Military Police school at Fort Gordon, Georgia.

His two friends were to train elsewhere and he would miss them. As he stood in the seemingly eternal rain he noticed a small disturbance rippling through the ranks. A message was being relayed and he was surprised no officer seemed to notice and use it as an excuse to dress the miscreants down. When it reached John a quiver ran through him.

"A jeep accident in the night. Two NCOs in hospital, another one dead."

"Which sergeants?" John whispered back.

"Ours," said the whisperer. "The red haired one. Dead."

The soldier next to him was already passing the message on but John couldn't have repeated it. He felt one big lump of grief for the sergeant he had almost liked. Never even got to Vietnam. Poor bastard.

"John, gotta go." Ben, his Eskimo face serious, held out his hand.

"Move it, Davison," ordered an NCO.

John's hand brushed his friend's then they saluted each other and as they were each pushed toward a different waiting bus Ben's face broke into its old familiar grin. "See you in Nam," he shouted.

CHAPTER SIX
Moving On

The mood was very different on this bus from the one coming up from San Francisco to Washington. Those recruits had seemed like a bunch of scared kids, these were exuberant, relishing freedom after surviving twelve weeks of hell. They joked amongst each other and John joined in. Now they had something in common; they were all headed to Military police school which each must have professed interest in to be assigned it now.

The ride to Seattle airport was short and a plane was waiting on the runway when they arrived. One soldier stopped at the top of the steps and looked up into the rain which as usual pelted down from the lowering sky. "Goodbye Washington and to hell with your f…in' weather! We're headin' into the sun shine," and he ducked inside. Everyone cheered and followed him.

John scrambled into a window seat and looked out to see all their duffel bags being loaded into the cargo hold below. He couldn't tell which was his—they all looked the same. He scanned the seats around him. All these guys looked the same too—even though they were wearing their own jeans and windbreakers. John decided it was their identical shaved heads. His too. Except for skin color how would someone recognize him among the dead of a battlefield? A wave of homesickness overwhelmed him as he thought of dying and being left in some foreign place. I don't want that, he moaned inwardly and found his hands had grasped the dog tag around his neck.

"May I take that, please, sir?" A pretty young stewardess pointed to the guitar John had protected, but not played, since he left home. "It'll be safe up front."

He gave it to her and watched until it was safely placed behind a curtain in the galley.

The plane took off. Someone cheered as two stewardesses passed out beer and sandwiches. A party mood progressed with the seemingly endless cans of Coors and John's morbid thoughts disappeared. A cheer went up and he twisted to see that the stewardess who had taken his guitar was now in the lap of the soldier who had said goodbye to the rain earlier. They seemed to be getting on really well.

John took another swig and joined in the merriment. Bootcamp with its endless hours of harassment, marching weary and soaked, feeling stressed to breaking; all finished. He was free. Soon he'd be on his way to fighting for his country and becoming a hero. John crushed the empty beer can in his right hand and reached out for another with his left.

CHAPTER SEVEN
Augusta, Georgia

When John stepped out of the plane it was as though someone threw a steaming hot blanket over his head. And this was evening! They were hustled onto a bus and had gone no more than half a mile when someone vomited. The smell permeated the vehicle and John regretted all those beers he'd had which threatened a reappearance at any moment.

He didn't remember much more of that evening

He awoke with a splitting headache, being rousted at four thirty the next morning from a bunk he hardly remembered getting into. He'd only just gotten dressed in fresh fatigues when the order came to line up outside for inspection. Even this early the muggy heat had him sweating and his lungs struggling to find oxygen.

He had trouble focusing on the NCO's red face that appeared too close to his own. "We expect spit shine here, Soldier." He pointed to John's boots. "KP next time."

"Sir." John snapped to attention and saluted.

The Sergeant moved on to the next in line.

John now realized how wrong they'd all been yesterday in rejoicing that boot camp was over. Being here was much worse. First came sixty two hours of sleep deprivation.

It began that night about the time of expected "lights out" which never came; instead John was sent to clean the latrines then, after inspection, ordered to reclean. After another inspection he was sent outside to rake the gravel "so it wouldn't get caught in the General's tires". At first John was angry, getting madder and madder as the hot night wore on. Then he was just tired but as soon as he paused, leaned against a wall to rest, someone was yelling "Move it Davison, this isn't no shitass holiday camp. Get a bucket and wash these here windows. Move it!" John didn't even care that someone else had just finished washing them.

This is to toughen me, he kept telling himself, so I'll be a good American soldier. Gotto stick it out or I'll feel ashamed of myself forever after.

And so it went hour after hour until dawn. Then for a few moments the men were allowed to sit for breakfast but John had no interest in food, all he wanted was sleep and he would have dropped off right then except for the watchful eyes and threats of the fresh NCOs who John noticed had taken over from his nighttime torturers.

His platoon was herded out to the parade ground and made to stand at attention as the sun rose to bake them. Several recruits passed out but were immediately wrenched to their feet and slapped awake. They set out on a forced march and John moved in a daze, then they stood some more. So hot. So tired. And angry. He'd about kill to sleep

Evening came. All he could do in the mess hall was drink water. Did it never cool off down here? Black waves of panic almost overcame him as he was kept moving all that day and the next hot night. Some faces seemed to be missing. Had they gone AWOL? Maybe he should too, if only there wasn't that stronger fear of failure. He would do almost anything just to sleep but there was always a fresh Sergeant on his tail, yelling at him to keep going, do meaningless chores when all he wanted was his bed. He would die out here. He wasn't even mad anymore. Just that sinking, despairing craving for sleep.

Day melded into night. John noticed that the men around him looked old with sunken eyes. He must look the same. Another march—if you could call it that—more chores. He saw no end to this torture and had no reaction when late that afternoon they were dismissed and told to eat then go to their bunks.

It must be a trick. John was afraid to believe it. He went straight to his bunk and crashed to know nothing for 16 hours.

After a cold shower and a good breakfast, John was optimistic, even exhilarated, as if he had completed a marathon in which the last five miles had been agony. But he had crossed the finish line! After all what could they do to him that was worse than that nightmare of sleeplessness? He could handle anything the army threw at him. He was ready for Vietnam.

There were many vacancies on the parade ground. Rumor had it some men had had nervous breakdowns and were in hospital. When John looked around, most of his platoon buddies looked shaky with dark rings around their eyes and John was proud to be feeling pretty chipper considering...That is until a few miles into the long march. Then things started swimming in front of his eyes and at one point he staggered out of formation and sagged against a tree. Someone gave him a drink of water and he took the bottle and poured it over his head, holding his face up to it. This heat was a killer. He grabbed another bottle and drank it all as he was hustled back into line.

As they marched they chanted. "The Cong came marching over the hill.

Baroom, Baroom.

And we'll all be dead by this time next year.

Baroom, Baroom."

Christ, are they really making us sing that! thought John.

The soldier on his right nudged him and John glanced over to see it was Greg, the one who'd made out with the stewardess in the plane.

Greg winked at him. "Don't worry, kid," he said out of the side of his mouth "We'll kick ass here yet." Then he bellowed out the last line changed to:

"And we'll all be home by Summer next year.
Baroom, Baroom."
John, loudly picked up on it and soon everyone was singing the revised version. If the Sergeants noticed they showed no sign.

That night after supper they were actually allowed free time. Some of the men went to bed but, although tired, John wandered into the common room where a few of his troop sat around glumly reading magazines or dozing while a VT mumbled from a rack on the wall. Were these dull looking people the same as those who had been so full of fun and energy on the plane?

An idea came to him, one that wiped his sleepy mind clear and sent him hurrying back to his locker. A few moments later he strolled through the door of the common room strumming his guitar and singing, "This little light of mine..."

The men looked up.

"I'm gonna let it shine"

They began to smile and then joined in. John flashed back to similar happy times in college and he played the next verse. Everyone was singing now. A sergeant looked in. Watched for a moment, shook his head and left.

John's heart pounded as he led from song to song. For the first time since leaving home he was truly happy and doing what he did best, making others laugh at his goofy humor and sweeping everyone along with his music so they completely forgot the misery of the previous days.

In the end every soldier slapped him on the back as, grinning, they left for their bunks; and John that night slept as though no army or Viet Cong existed.

Next day they marched to the range for target practice with the M16. John enjoyed that, hitting the bulls eye every time, which disgusted the NCO by giving him no excuse to scream at this recruit as he did the others.

After lunch they were sent to crawl with their rifles through thick brush. John cursed the sodden heat and the myriad bugs which attacked any speck of flesh they could find. He stood up once to shake them off and a bullet whizzed close over his head making him drop back to the ground. He imagined the NCO grinning about that one. One guy near him whimpered for fear of the snakes that were said to inhabit the area. To hell with snakes, thought John, it's our own bloody officer that's going to kill us!

He learned a lot during that first week—much of it from Greg who was always up to something and never got caught. For example—KP. The first time John was given that was for not having his spit shined boots glassy enough.

He'd never liked saunas and when he entered the kitchen he thought he was in one. Steam bubbled up from pots on the stove, while cook shouted orders. Banging and clanking added to the tumult and John gasped for breath as he peeled countless potatoes.

"I musta lost ten pounds! I thought I was going to die in there," he told Greg afterwards.

Greg stopped peeling the bark off a twig with the penknife he always carried and looked up. "Well, don't do it. Never see me doing KP do ya?"

"No. but how…?"

"Pay someone else to do it for you. Twenty bucks usually does it and Cook doesn't know one of us from the other."

And with that advice and a stack of dwindling twenty dollar bills John never did KP again.

That second week in Georgia was packed with long marches in the heat, continuous inspections during which he always seemed to be singled out to do push ups for some failure or other. Mainly he felt he'd never had a chance to catch up on those first days of sleeplessness and when he did sleep he often had nightmares in which he relived the horror of the experience.

He could hardly believe it when he heard on Sunday that they were free to go into Augusta. As soon as he got off the bus John, guitar slung over his shoulder, headed straight for what seemed like heaven; a room in a good hotel with the most comfortable bed in the world, two six packs of frosty beer, and a TV for later. First he had a very long shower after which he dived in between crisp, cool sheets and was droned to sleep by the hum of the air conditioner.

When he awoke it was dusk outside and after shaving and drinking a beer he dressed in his clean Pendleton shirt and jeans. He was hungry. John felt like a new man.

There was a USO up the street and he wandered in, ordered another beer and a hamburger. After three girls in WAC uniforms sang, the mic was opened for anyone to perform. John, with his guitar, strode up and began to sing the Kingston Trio's hit song. "Hang down your head Tom Dooly" After a few bars his voice was strong again and the guitar, though slightly out of tune, felt perfect under his fingers. John filled with joy as the roomful of Gi's joined in and the room rocked with the sound. For three more songs John led the way and it seemed all the misery and belittling of the last months drained away and he was on top of the world.

"Time to go. Bus is outside." Someone was tapping him on the shoulder, bringing him down to earth with a bump.

Half an hour later, back in camp, John thought over the day. It had been good but best was that it had shown him that there was still real life going on not far away, with laughter and drink and music. It wasn't all misery and being yelled at as he had begun to believe. Those smiling, shining faces singing along had filled him with a wonderful joy and let him become the best of the real John Davison. He advised himself to remember that feeling and bring it out like a precious gem whenever he felt low. That night he slept without nightmares.

"Come on. Quick. Have some fun." Greg beckoned from the Latrine doorway where John had been left to scrub every inch to perfection or be made to "Push up Georgia" again until his arms collapsed.

Without questioning, John followed his friend to a waiting jeep but before they set off Greg took a wad of chewing gum from his mouth, ripped a piece of tin foil he pulled from his pocket into six strips; then with gum as a backing he stuck three on John's chest, three on his own. With a grin he stamped on the accelerator and they roared onto the road alongside the parade ground.

A battalion was just returning from a forced march and as they passed Greg saluted. John imitated him, busting with stifled laughter as the weary men, seeing Greg and John's lieutenant's bars, dutifully saluted back.

Around a corner they parked and, after a moment of doubled over hilarity, deserted the borrowed jeep and went their separate ways; John back to scrubbing latrines but with a grin that took a long time to fade.

He really expected to be caught and thrown in the brig next day but when nothing had happened by evening he relaxed. In fact he soon found that Greg led a magical life as he was never held accountable for any of his many escapades. Even the small marijuana plot he cultivated behind a storage shed was never discovered. Even after ingesting too many of his own version of cookies and passing out on the lawn, his being carried in and placed on his bunk by friends went unnoticed by the brass.

But John was impatient of being here, seemingly wasting time when there was a war to be won. Each night he drew a thick line through that date on his calendar until finally there was only one day left before going home for two weeks leave.

They lined up, each soldier tensely waiting to learn his fate. There were three possibilities: Germany, which many hoped for, Hawaii, which most of the others wanted, and of course, Vietnam.

They were chosen alphabetically and John was happy for Greg Black when he got Hawaii. Might the surname Davison be low enough for him to escape Vietnam. But wasn't 'Nam what he had signed up for in the first place? Wasn't going there what a patriot did? John held his breath, eyes riveted on the officer reading from his list. "Jerry Dancer, Vietnam. John Davison, Vietnam. George Du..."

John let out the breath he hadn't known he was holding.

Next morning they assembled on the parade ground for the last time and were dismissed for their two weeks leave.

Some men dressed in casual civvies while others, including John, wore their dress uniforms in which to go home. John knew it would please his mother to see how smart he looked and he himself was proud to be recognized as a member of the US forces.

Mum, Dad and Sis met him at Oakland airport. They all hugged him and chattered the local news to him on the drive home. It was then John realized that there was little he could tell them about what he had been through during his months away. Instead he complained about the bad food and how glad he was to be home to fill up on Mom's cooking and how much it rained in Seattle.

Those two weeks flew by. His mother hovered and cooked his favorite meals while Dad told stories and jokes he'd heard on his rounds as top Salesman of his company. Sis took off with her own teenage friends after the first few days and John refrained from mentioning the small recent dent he noticed in the yellow fender of his Chevy. Only his dog stuck by his side and together they roamed the tawny hillsides, creeks and woods of his childhood, relishing the silence only made richer by bird song and distant bawling of cattle.

He went to the soda fountain on main street and talked to the people he knew whose main interests seemed to be the weather and the new highway which was going to cut their small town in two. He wondered what Greg was doing... and his Eskimo buddy Ben.

On the radio and in headlines he learned of demonstrations against America's involvement in the Vietnam war. Some draft dodgers were even running up to Canada. Traitors and cowards, John thought and was glad of the choice he'd made. All these people would be proud to know him after the war was won and line up to hear his battle stories. Maybe he'd even write a song or two about it.

CHAPTER EIGHT

It seemed no time until John was back in his fatigues waving goodbye to his teary eyed parents and his sister who was fascinated by the Flying Tiger from whose door John gave a final wave. A moment later the plane raced down the runway and left land. A thud as the wheels retracted and he watched S.F. below growing smaller and smaller until there was only ocean and the hum of engines. At last he was off on the adventure he'd signed up for. He accepted a beer from the steward and looked around the cabin. All the men looked cheerful and eager for what was ahead, just as he was. Whatever their differences they wore the same uniform, belonged to the same "club." They'd be like brothers. John filled with warmth toward this new family.

The plane landed in Okinawa for an hour and John planned to see as much of the island as he could in that time. He heard others talking about renting taxis. Was Okinawa like the island in the musical "South Pacific"? His sister loved that movie.

At the top of the steps John paused to read the huge banner of welcome just this side of the adjacent plane.

SAYONARA—HAVE SAFE AND PLEASANT JOURNEY

Decent of them, thought John, then craned forward to see what all that activity was going on behind the great banner.

"Coffins," murmured the soldier behind him. "American soldiers going home."

John's gaze clung to those shining metal containers holding bodies of boys who, just like him, had not long ago gone to war with visions of becoming patriotic heroes. He felt a lump of sadness in his stomach. Now they would have neither children nor grandkids to speak of them with pride. Was he looking at the end of his own future out there on this Okinawa airfield? Was every man with him thinking the same thing? No one spoke... and no one left the airport but sat silently for the hour until their next flight was ready for boarding. When it was, they all kept their eyes averted from the sign wishing them a safe and pleasant trip—and what might be going on behind it.

As he again occupied his window seat John wondered if everyone was as scared as he was. Sure, he'd thought of death when he signed up but always in the abstract not like the too real, all encompassing, cloud of fear seeing those coffins had produced. The plane's engines hummed carrying each of its passengers to his inescapable fate.

Christ! John's gaze focused outside on a black oily substance oozing onto the wing. For a moment he watched it grow, more rapidly now. "Stewardess!" he called

The Stewardess' practiced smile faded as her eyes followed John's pointing finger then, without a word, she sprinted up the aisle and into the pilot's cabin. A few seconds later a voice announced their return to Okinawa due to a minor hydraulic malfunction.

We could have crashed and died right here without even getting to Vietnam. thought John. Ya never know what you're gonna get.

After a safe landing they were given a three day leave and amidst whoops of joy the whole troop headed for the nearest bar.

John had no recollection of what he did during those three days and was eternally grateful to whoever got him back to the plane on time. He slept, dreamlessly until a Steward awoke him with a very welcome cup of steaming coffee. "We will be landing at Biên Hòa in ten minutes," he said.

As the engines quieted and they began the long descent a gasp travelled around the plane. Everyone was looking out his window, and each face was stained a bloody red.

John put down his cup, pulled his own curtain back and caught his breath. It was as though he had opened the door to a furnace. The whole of Vietnam airspace glowed a shocking crimson, and clouds writhed as though stained with gore The plane became part of the picture as it dove toward the landing strip. Several soldiers crossed themselves and John thought he would too—if he were Catholic.

CHAPTER NINE

They deplaned into muggy early evening stillness and gathered on the tarmac watching silently as their duffel bags were taken from the hold and loaded onto a trolley.

An engine's roar split the silence and a Jeep screeched to a stop in front of them. A stocky Sergeant jumped out and saluted, "Welcome to Vietnam!"

"Oh, Christ!" John muttered as an explosion somewhere too close rocked the ground under his feet.

"Move it men! On the run 'less you wannabe target for a sniper's bullet. Buses are over there." The sergeant waved a hand toward a dark line of trees at the far edge of the air field. "On the double." Another explosion nearby added emphasis to the command and forty-odd young soldiers sprinted, in spite of the heat and heavy boots, toward where several decrepit buses waited.

Already soaked with sweat and straining to find oxygen in the heavy air, John collapsed onto the bus's seat. A small mousy looking man who John thought should be working in an accountant's office, slid in next to him.

"Bummer," he said to John with the ghost of a grin.

"Bummer," grunted John as the bus jolted off already at full throttle.

It was dark now and as they passed through a village John peered out, fascinated by the ramshackle huts that lined the narrow road. Inside he saw families hunkered in candle light and he wondered what they talked about—what they were eating. It all looked very peaceful.

After what seemed a long time on a bone jolting road the bus entered a gate and stopped in front of a barracks. Dog tired John followed others into a room lined with bunks five beds high, flung himself into a lower one and, still fully dressed, slept.

An explosion nearby woke him. Tense, he waited. He looked at his watch. One AM. More distant gunfire periodically punctured the noise of insects and creatures he didn't recognize. A mosquito hummed and landed on his arm. He slapped it and didn't know if he got it or not. He slept.

"John! John!" His mother was calling from the kitchen where she was making breakfast. Soon Sis would be up to drag him out of bed.

A loud crash. What the hell had Ma dropped! John opened his eyes to darkness. He couldn't possibly be in Vietnam. Not possibly! Just Private—not John anymore...

Snores came from different areas of the darkness. He hadn't known there were so many different kinds, from bass to falsetto. A whimper. Was someone crying?

John curled on his side and tried to shut it all out. One sheep, two. Did they have sheep in Vietnam?

Next morning he washed the sweat off himself under a tepid, swamp smelling shower. As he shaved, a creature seeming as large as a small bird flew onto the mirror. Crouching on his reflected cheek the praying mantis reared up and stared at him. John stared back. He'd seen them back home but never this big. The size and number of bugs here was disconcerting. Odd they were so big and the people so small. He finished shaving, washed the soap off his face, and left before the insect could reappear.

Breakfast was rice and fish washed down with coffee and, as he was hungry, unable to remember when he last ate, John went back for more until he realized his coffee smelled the same as his earlier shower and he wasn't hungry anymore.

Lined up in a walled area under the already baking sun they were given orders for the day. Grunt work. The Sergeant finished by again warning about snipers. "They can be anywhere. Last night one of the men who came in with you was on guard duty. They got him between the eyes. Remember those gooks are everywhere. Every second you are in Nam you are a target. Every second. Now get to your duties."

John vaguely remembered one of their group being assigned guard duty. Poor bastard. He tried to remember the kid's face but couldn't. Only been in Vietnam a few hours. Now maybe in one of those coffins at Okinawa waiting for a plane home. Oh, shit!

He worked heaving boxes into a supply room all day and guessed he must have sweated off twenty pounds by the time they broke for supper.

A Captain spoke after they had finished eating but still sat at the long tables, many of them smoking cigarettes. "I have something very important to say and for you men to remember, We are in someone else's country helping them stop Communism from taking over. We Americans are here to protect these good people. It is important that each one of us always shows respect to them and their customs. Do nothing that could hurt our country's reputation. Be proud that you, America's finest, represent the United States of America."

From somewhere a tinny recording began to play, "God bless America, Land of the free, Home of the Brave..." The men all stood and John felt tears fill his throat and his whole body flood with patriotism. This was why he had joined up. He had almost forgotten.

That night at a general assembly he and one other soldier were told they had been assigned as guards at Long Binh Prison and would be transported there the next day. The voice continued to announce the combat units others would join but John heard none of it as he stood frozen in shock. A guard? There must be a mistake. Rumors had circulated about LBJ, nickname for the infamous prison for American soldiers who had committed crimes, but he was trained for combat. No one got medals for being a prison guard. What war stories could he tell his kids? What would his parents and buddies back home think? Now he wouldn't even be with these guys he was already beginning to bond with.

As he lay in his bunk later he decided not to tell his parents until he had to. No point in disillusioning them. He would write about the continuous rumble of gunfire he already heard from the enemy that was all around them and could shoot at any time of day or night. That at least was true!

John slept fitfully. until an enormous explosion sent him hurtling off his mattress. What the hell! Panicked, he grabbed the rail connecting his bunk to the one above and hung on to it for dear life. Everything went quiet. Sheepishly, still shaking, he loosened his grip and prayed, "Please don't let anyone see me like this!" At that moment, to his horror, the overhead lights flashed on. When he dared look around he saw that almost every soldier in the barracks had reacted as he had and probably felt as embarrassed.

A sergeant appeared in the doorway. "That was outgoing fire earlier," he said. "One enemy mortar just got through. Not much damage. Thought you'd like to know." His face wore a broad grin as he looked around, then the lights clicked off.

CHAPTER TEN

Next morning, already sweating, John and a baby-faced Pvt. Olsen tossed duffels and everything else they owned, into the back of a Jeep. Then they climbed in next to the driver who, as they roared off, shouted his name as Corporal Stack. John got the feeling he considered himself much superior to his raw recruit passengers which on second thought he actually was—in fact everyone seemed to be his superior lately.

But John didn't care; he didn't want to talk anyway. Avoiding the large crack in the windshield he leaned out to the side and got the full blast of air in his face. It was hot but at least air.

He pulled back in, annoyed at Olsen who was digging him in the ribs. "What the hell's matter with..."

His attention turned from Olsen to the Corporal who was bellowing, "Get your fucking head in lest you want it blown off."

John looked around. They were speeding down a dirt highway with barren fields stretching on either side. "Nowhere for a sniper to hide here," he shouted back.

"Not snipers, land mines, Asshole."

Yikes, thought John, why the heck doesn't he slow down then and as though reading his mind the corporal continued. "I figure driving the faster the better—if we hit one maybe we'll leave the blast behind. Others don't agree but that's what I do and I ain't dead yet."

John, during the next four barren miles, saw the remains of several vehicles piled up at the side of the road but he kept his head in and made himself believe that maybe going faster was better.

Then there it was, a high metal wall and they were headed to the only break in the whole forbidding edifice. A huge metal door swung open then clanged shut behind them manned by armed guards. John felt the whole world he knew disappear behind him. 'Give up hope all ye who enter here.' Where had he read those words? But they sure seemed appropriate right now.

The jeep braked.

"I'll dump your duffels at the hooch. You dismount here!"

John and Olsen jumped out and stood at attention, saluting the Sergeant who had appeared to greet them. Behind him John heard the jeep start up and roar back out the gate which he heard shut with a clang of finality.

He looked around and felt his skin crawl. Cell blocks loomed at the back of yards enclosed in high cage-like fencing topped with concertina wire. Inside, prisoners lolled smoking or watching with desultory interest. Heat bounced off the ground.

The sergeant talked, providing basic orientation while he unlocked the gate into one of the compounds. These were mostly young white soldiers in for minor infractions, he explained. "But never turn your back on a prisoner. Don't forget they all hate you and figure they have nothing to lose. We're understaffed and they know it." They went on into the wooden building containing cells where the men spent time when not let into the exercise yard.

John couldn't get out of there fast enough and felt like shaking himself as his dog had after a too close encounter with a skunk. There was something wrong here. He'd been in prisons before and they hadn't smelled like this. He sniffed, trying to decipher what it was. Fear. He recognized it now. The whole place reeked of it. At that moment his eye caught sudden movement some distance away in the next yard as a mountainous black man lunged toward a guard and smacked him across the face. To John's surprise the guard showed no retaliation; just walked away.

"Did you see that?" It burst out of him. "That guard did nothing. The prisoner hit him!"

"You learn to pick your fights here, Soldier!" snapped Sergeant "They'll take care of anything serious." He jerked his thumb upward.

John followed the officer's gesture to the guard towers placed at intervals along the top of the outer wall. In the two nearest he saw rifles aimed toward the aggressive prisoner who had already melted in among his fellows.

"Now Private Collins will give you the rest of the grand tour." Sergeant bolted the door of the Yard behind them then pointed toward the flatbed truck that had drawn up alongside. It was driven by one of the guards who had let them in earlier at the main gate and after the obligatory salutes John and Olsen climbed aboard the flat surface while the Sergeant sped off in his jeep.

Collins drove slowly to enable the two rooky guards to look through the fencing at the prisoners who crowded to look back. They were separated into groups as to seriousness of their crime, smoking a joint to murder, but they all looked bitter and desperate. Many swore and spat at them and John wondered if this was a daily happening. He remembered being at the San Francisco zoo once, looking in at the caged monkeys and laughing at their antics. Now he felt miserable, the situation no different, but these were men.

"Here." The driver had reached behind himself and taken two rocks from a small pile there. He handed one to John. "Throw it at them," he said while, as an example and with practiced aim, he caused blood to spurt from a skinny dark skinned face. "Black Panthers; killers. Most on lockdown. Hate everyone white. Other prisoners. Everyone."

John had wondered why that pile of stones was in the corner. Now he knew and dropped the one in his hand, letting it roll off onto the road. Not even a Black Panther…

The guard looked at him a moment. "After a few months you won't feel like that." And he threw another which missed its quarry, hitting a metal post and dropping to the ground.

God, please don't let me lose my humanity, John fervently prayed to a deity he had previously only pretended to believe in to keep his parents happy.

What am I doing here about to guard American young men, who are kept like animals in a zoo? Viet Cong I was ready for, not this.

"And this is Big Red." The guard's voice broke into his reverie. "This is the end of your ride." They were in a remote corner of the stockade facing mountains of sand. "Fill bags 'til chow. Someone'll show you where to eat and after, take you through the gate to your hooch across the way."

The truck left.

John and Olsen looked at each other.

"Scary place," said Olsen. "Something bad about it."

"Like a powder keg ready to blow." John rubbed the back of his neck, and spat the metallic taste out of his mouth. "Better stuff sacks. What the hell for, expecting a flood maybe?"

And so they sweated in their own breathless, sweltering corner of hell.

They got a break when a guard came by and told them, while pointing the way to the mess hall, to go get chow. John was surprised to find that they were to eat in the same place as the prisoners but was relieved to learn that they had eaten earlier and were now locked back in their own areas.

As soon as he walked in he felt the hair rise on the back of his neck and his stomach turn at the smell of sweat, anger and misery left behind. How could he ever eat in here! But when he lined up with the other guards at the hatch and received his plate of mashed potatoes with gravy, a big patty of hamburger and some kind of green vegetable, he forgot everything except how hungry he was. Finding an empty place at one of the tables he dove into the food and thought of nothing else until he finished his second helping. The room was quiet but for the clink of utensils. John would have liked to ask questions but as no one seemed inclined to talk he concentrated on his coffee.

"Okay, Private, back to the sandbags," an officer barked at his elbow.

Wearily he stood and went back to work sweating and beating off bugs that threatened to eat him alive. What on earth did they want with all these sandbags anyway? John was too weary to even complain to his workmate who probably felt as bad as he did. When someone came to relieve them and take them out through the metal gate to the outside world it felt no cooler nor less oppressive than inside the stockade. Across a road and inside the cement building acting as barracks that he was already calling a hooch, John, after the most cursory wash, fell onto the bunk assigned him and was instantly asleep.

CHAPTER ELEVEN
LBJ

Wailing sirens! Explosions! What the hell? John scrambled upright and stood dazed, confused. Flames flared and gyrated over the walls. "Fire! Fire! Riot! They've set the stockade on fire! Collect your weapons!" The messenger raced through the dorm to be heard still shouting in the distance as crimson flared and the night turned into a raging furnace. John grabbed his clothes and, still pulling on his shirt, joined the other bodies jostling toward the door. Once outside each soldier paused hypnotized by the flaming horror across the street then set off at full run to where John discovered they were giving out weapons. An M14, ammo and bayonet were thrust into his hands and as he hurtled back into the street he cursed his ineptitude at affixing his bayonet and loading his weapon at a flat run. After several tries he managed it. Close to the inferno, he stopped, watching flames lick the barbed wire at the top of the stockade wall from inside.

Mingling with the fire's roar were the shouts and screams of men whose silhouettes appeared high above, ready to jump. From the guard towers came the steady pop of shotguns. John stood paralyzed by the horror of it all.

"This way, Soldier, follow me." John did. Flickering shadows made it hard to see; men, dark shapes, ran in all directions. Roaring, crackling, screams and commands interspersed with gunfire. Sergeant held up his hands. "Wait here! Shoot any man who climbs over. No prisoner can touch ground. You hear me, Private?" He shouted into John's face. Then he was gone leading the other men farther on.

John stood alone in the chaos, rifle aimed upward. Smoke made it hard to breathe and stung his eyes. One thing I do know, he thought, I am not going to kill an American. At that moment he saw three dark shapes clambering over the wall above him. "Go back!" His voice was a hoarse roar. "You land outside we've orders to shoot! Go back you suckers! Get the hell back!" Please, he whispered to himself.

A pause followed during which everything seemed to stop; all sound and time waited and John held his breath.

It seemed forever—then the prisoners slid back out of sight and John almost dropped his weapon with relief. Yet what awaited them in there? Had he sent them back to be incinerated or murdered by one of the vicious leaders of the revolt? Here he was in a position of power, chooser of life or death, yet he had never felt so helpless.

A chopper circled overhead sweeping the area with its searchlight; thumping the night with its sound. No color now, as wall and guard towers stood out in stark black and white. Even the voices around him seemed muted. The night throbbed with rage and pain; smelled of smoke, sweat and terror.

"C'mon, Move it." A sergeant whapped him on the back and he turned to follow.

At the gate John, with others, was ordered to stand guard outside as officers marched on in. The camp commander led the way and John watched through the opening as the CO motioned for those with him to stand to one side and wait. Alone the CO walked forward to face the crowd of rebellious prisoners. John couldn't make out the words as he began to speak in a tone conciliatory, almost pleading. John stopped breathing, surprised at what he was hearing. These were not children to be cajoled into good behavior! These, at the moment, were enraged animals. What was the man thinking? And John remembered his surprise on that previous day when the guard walked away from being slapped in the face by a prisoner. The Commander was still speaking but beneath it John heard a rumble and then a roar as the prisoners charged at full run toward what they perceived in the dim light as the open gate behind him.

John watched in amazement as they knocked flat, then ran right over the CO now invisible under the churning feet of the escaping convicts. John had to stifle an uncontrollable urge to laugh. His last sight as the metal gate clanged shut between him and them was of the guards already inside stepping forward with their bayonets drawn and the onslaught of hopeful escapees skidding to a stop.

Nobody spoke. All were tense, listening. John looked up at the guard towers and in the early light of dawn saw each was armed now with shotguns trained on the compound below.

A sudden yank on his shirt caught him off balance, sent him hurtling backward and crashing to the ground. "What the…!?" Something like a striking snake just missed his face. He struggled to his feet and turned to fight off his attacker.

"Cool it, Man."

John recognized the big black guy from the bunk across the aisle he'd noticed when they'd been rousted from sleep—it seemed a lifetime ago. The soldier was pointing to something and when John looked he saw what he had taken for a snake had sparks sputtering from it.

"Electric wire broke loose. Woulda fried you," the big man said.

For a moment John couldn't speak then he filled with gratitude, "You saved my life. Thanks. I sure owe you!"

A shout came from somewhere inside, snapping the waiting men into alert attention. When nothing followed they relaxed. John's savior lit a limp cigarette. "Ya know I really hoped to kill one of them maggots," he said exhaling the words with a cloud of smoke.

"Why?" said John surprised.

"Then they'd send me home," The private spat a flake of tobacco toward the ground.

What a crazy upside down world this Vietnam was. A man could save a stranger one minute and hope to kill another stranger the next. But, John thought, for him even the chance to go home wouldn't be worth killing someone for. God, I hope I never get like that.

The sun was now scorching as they waited hungry and weary and stressed. Nobody seemed to want to talk and John's thoughts drifted to the hills of California and his mother's pancakes.

"Line up. Men. We're headin' in!"

Everyone jumped to attention. They were marched into the stockade, back to the entrance of Big Red where it seemed a lifetime since John had spent miserable hours there filling sandbags. Now they were told the leaders of the uprising were holed up in there refusing to come out.

John and the other guards were formed into two lines evidently for the recaptured prisoners to walk between after a negotiator talked them into surrendering.

"Weapons ready. One wrong move, shoot 'em!" roared the officer.

John sited along the barrel of his M14 right into the eyes of the soldier opposite him. He lowered his weapon. "Sir! Sir!"

"What is it Private?" The officer strode to John's side.

"If we shoot we'll kill each other, Sir!"

The sergeant's eyes were stones. "Be cool, Davison," was all he said and moved back by the gate to welcome the jeep that had just arrived.

The men all saluted the Major who passed between them and disappeared, striding into the area which held the rebellious prisoners. John wondered at his show of bravado He must be either crazy or very brave.

It seemed a long time that they stood there at attention. Sergeant barked at any man he perceived as wilting and John was grateful for each episode that relieved the boredom.

"Here they come!" Someone nearest the door said it.

"Weapons ready!" ordered Sergeant.

John winced at thought of the one pointed at him and made sure his own aim was off to the left of his opposite's shoulder. Please make that soldier as good a sharpshooter and as aware as I am, he prayed.

Then they came. A bedraggled group of prisoners—terrified and exhausted. Some with blood on their clothes. Nearly all variations of white with a few blacks who hadn't gone along with the racial agenda.

The Major came last looking drained but triumphant having negotiated a deal with the riot's leaders to at least let those leave who wanted to.

John helped shepherd them through the burned remains of the stockade to enclosures where they seemed relieved to be shut in behind the concertina wire, safe from their tormentors.

'Here, put these two by themselves." A sergeant had come up and left him with two prisoners different from the rest. Tall and ebony and mean. He'd seen guys like them in Oakland. One stopped abruptly and stared down at him. "Us black Panthers are goin' to get you one of these days white boy."

John glared back feeling pure anger crawl through him. "That's just fine," he snarled, releasing his weapon's safety with a loud click.

The Panther dragged a cigarette from his pocket and bent over to pick up a still smoldering ember to use as a light .

John trained his rifle on the man. "No." his trigger figure was oh so ready. Deadlocked they stood until, slowly the big black dropped the ember and looked away.

"Get!" John ordered, directing the prisoners into an adjoining enclosure in which their burned out cell block and only shade still smoldered. He locked the gate solidly behind him and as he strode away thought he heard the mostly white, prisoners in the next yard breathe a sigh of relief. Some gave him respectful nods as he passed and, as most were still drinking deeply from the water barrels, John promised refills and told them food would be brought soon although secretly he wasn't sure how that would happen as there seemed little left of any buildings on the fort.

Alone, he noticed he was trembling and leaned against a post for support. As the conflicting emotions of moments before threatened to overwhelm him, John realized that for the first time he could have killed an American and felt good about it. In those few minutes he had learned that whatever the race, an enemy was an enemy and had to be dealt with. Now he knew he could do it.

Along with his growth of confidence there was also an enormous sadness as he realized he'd forever lost part of himself—his innocence. John ducked into a nearby latrine until he could return to his unit with emotions in check.

John thought the change in him must show on his face as he joined the rest back at Big Red but they were too busy pulling a body from inside the door to notice him at all. Its head was red pulp and John turned away. Sergeant handed out smoke grenades, "These'll rout 'em." And he tossed his toward the back where the rebellion's instigators still hung out. Men began coughing as smoke drifted their way.

"Sir?"

"Yes, Davison,"

"Isn't that the storeroom in there, sir?"

"What of it Davison?" then loudly, "Get ready to throw, Men!"

"Won't they have gas masks in there, Sir? We don't, Sir!"

"Hold it!"

But some soldiers had already thrown their bombs and smoke was billowing back out at them, causing ferocious coughing and gagging. Others hastily covered their noses and turned away, while the door clanged shut.

"You're a trouble maker, Davison," Sergeant said before giving the order to stand strong, as though expecting panicked prisoners to be smoked out in spite of John's information.

Adrenalin had kept everyone going throughout the long hours but now heat and weariness siphoned the life out of them.

"How d'you think they're going to get those guys out of there?" John asked a soldier next to him.

The man, boy really by the look of the fuzz on his face, spat and shrugged, "Thirst, hunger. One'll decide it for them."

"They must be cooking in there already. Bad enough out here." Most of the men had opened their shirts, which were dark with sweat soaked soot.

"Big, black dudes can take a lot. Hey, look, Sarge is giving us a break."

"Thank God!"

Trucks had arrived with food from Saigon and, leaving the compound with its smoldering destruction and fetid smells, John's squad slogged across the road to their quarters and the ultimate pleasure of food, beer and sleep.

As he faded into oblivion John heard voices joking and laughing. New Yorkers he thought recognizing the accent, they can joke about anything.

CHAPTER TWELVE

When he awoke next morning it was with a hollow scared feeling deep inside that had never been there before. He lay listening for the cries of terror and roar of fire but the only sound was of a rooster crowing. John vaguely remembered hearing throughout the night the sound of vehicles arriving and leaving the gate of the stockade across the way. He shook off the remnants of sleep and showered and dressed wondering where they'd eat with the mess hall burned to ash.

"Coffee in the common room, pass the word," said someone and he went down to find large urns and poured himself a mug of the brew which tasted good whatever it was.

"John Davison here?" A corporal stood in the doorway holding a box with US stamps.

"Davison here," he said hardly believing there was actually mail for him from home.

The others in the room surrounded him as he ripped off the brown paper. Everyone took a deep breath of the rich and wonderful fragrance that exuded from an inner box which John opened to find crammed full of his favorite chocolate chip cookies. It brought home so close he could imagine his mother smiling at him over the batch she'd just pulled from the oven. It brought tears to his eyes and he joked around so no one would notice. Suddenly he was the most popular guy on base and everyone acted a bit crazy, letting off steam after all the recent tension. John recited a poem he made up on the spur of the moment about how Sergeants didn't get cookies no more. Soon they were all laughing and John stuffed letters from his Mom, Dad and sister into his pocket to read later not caring that the box was almost empty and he'd only had a couple for himself.

All the while trucks were pouring in and out of the stockade. Tents were set up in their yards to house the low security detainees, while steel conexes were put in for the high security prisoners

John had seen those shipping containers on the Oakland docks and shuddered to think of men being shut up in them. They'd be like ovens, literally.

The soldier he voiced his concern to just shrugged. "They'll be let out into their yard for a while in the daytime, 'Sides, was them as caused the fire that burned their quarters. Let 'em cook."

John stood, chilled although dripping with sweat. I hate this place he thought. And this is only my second day.

It was then he noticed something odd about the shoulder of the private next to him and realized he had seen the same lump on the shoulders of many of the men who had been living here for a while. Before now he'd been too busy or tired to pay attention but now he looked closely into the little old man's wizened face and big brown eyes looking back at him.

The soldier laughed. "That's Amos," he said. "Most of us have pet monkeys. Buy 'em from the natives. Keeps us sane among all the crackpots we gotto deal with."

John watched as the small hands took something from the soldier and stuffed it into its mouth. " Coconut. Got it from the jungle. He likes apples and banana best but mess hasn't had them for a few days."

John decided he was going to get one of the cute creatures for himself as soon as things settled down, now he had to report for duty.

This proved to be guarding the familiar entrance to big Red where leaders of the previous night's riot still refused to give up. He was pleased to see that one of the guards on duty with him was a decent looking kid who'd eaten his fair share of cookies that morning. He was also one of the few who had thanked John for sharing. As the hours wore on they talked about home and both agreed that Vietnam, and LBJ especially, was hell. John felt better. Roger, as he introduced himself, already seemed a friend; someone he could talk to.

Around midnight an odd noise erupted from the depths of the building.

"What the?"

"Drums?" said John.

Both soldiers crept forward, weapons drawn, until they could see farther inside. They were dancing! Big black guys dressed like Swahili warriors. Two of them banged on metal buckets and they all grunted and shone with sweat. Lights were on but faded in and out, a makeshift power source causing a grotesque and unreal setting. Mesmerized John and Roger watched and soon John's foot began to tap to the rhythm.

After a while Roger nodded back to where they were supposed to be guarding.

"Wow!" said John a few seconds later.

"Wow!" replied Roger.

They both listened for a long time until the drumming stopped.

For five weeks those prisoners stayed holed up but they never danced again which disappointed John who spent long boring hours guarding the entrance each night. Intermittently several would appear showing signs of willingness to cooperate. Haggard and sullen they were taken away to be flown back to the States and Fort Leavenworth. John almost admired the stubbornness of the few who remained at the end, it must have been terrible in there with only rotting food, and stinking heat.

A new colonel arrived to take over the prison and immediately the mood changed as he snapped out orders and disciplined those who weren't quick to obey.

This officer's nickname quickly became Wyatt Earp to some, Ivan the terrible to others, but John liked him for his first command which was to get those men out of Big Red. Gas masks were promptly distributed and on John's watch the guards stormed in after tossing tear gas ahead of themselves. The few remaining renegades staggered out, gasping for breath, filthy and ragged, rubbing their eyes. John wondered if they were glad of the excuse to surrender but when he saw them being herded into the metal box in the top security pen he cringed at how stifling hot it would be in there, probably worse than the hell they had just left.

These instigators of the rebellion however were promptly handcuffed, shackled and flown back to the States to be incarcerated at Fort Leavenworth while their followers remained to suffer at LBJ.

Things changed under the new Colonel and John was assigned to work in the office, reviewing papers of new arrivals as they came in: some for such a minor crime as smoking marijuana, others for murder of a fellow soldier. All were hollow eyed and stooped from weariness, most limping from the pain of feet rotting in jungle-wet boots.

Some looked terrified, some belligerent, but John would not have felt safe near most of them without his weapon. There were a few young scared kids and those he tried to console by telling them LBJ was not as bad as its reputation, although he knew it really was. Instructed how to strip search he soon did it automatically. He was however bothered by the roughness of his coworker, a young private, Smit, who seemed permanently angry and took it out on the detainees, knocking them about and degrading them with threats and racial insults.

One afternoon John, working on papers at his desk, was growing more and more aggravated by the constant background of Smits's swearing at the prisoner he was presently questioning. Suddenly the sound changed as the young victim, a wiry black kid, turned on his inquisitor with a solid punch to the face and continued with all the viciousness learned on inner city streets. John leapt in, landing on the prisoner's back and in the process of trying to yank the two men apart fell against the door, bursting it open. Now outside, the struggle drew the attention of prisoners in the nearby block who gathered along the fence, cheering their "brother" on, many attempting to climb over to help.

Guards came running to separate the combatants. John stood back, relieved as in his imagination he had seen the fence breaking and the mob descending on him. Now he watched as they hauled the detainee away. But it wasn't him, John suddenly realized, it was Smit they'd mistaken for the villain! John, after a few seconds of soul searching, called after them and explained the mistake but also tried to get through to them how it was really Smit's fault for baiting the man. The guards, now holding the prisoner, just stared at John with blank disbelieving eyes

"Give the soldier a break. He's only in for a minor," John pleaded.

The kid had lost his fire and his shoulders slumped.

"Now let's go!" One guard said to the other. "We're done—get him out of here."

The prisoner hesitated, until John gave him a gentle shove.

He watched until the door closed behind the trio then turned to Smit who stood with blood streaming from his nose and his shirt ripped. "What the hell were you thinking!" he roared with all the frustration and anger of the past few moments. "That kid hadn't done anything to you. Besides he's bigger and way stronger. Are you crazy?"

To John's surprise Smit sank onto a chair and burst into loud rasping sobs. "It's alright for you!" The words came out in gasps. "You get letters from family and specially baked cookies. All the time you get them while I get nothing. I have a right to beat the crap out of any loser who comes in here."

John just stood, astonished, not knowing what to say. Awkwardly he sat at his typewriter and began to work on forms for the latest arrivals. He sensed the sobs change to nose blowing and then emptiness as Smit left the room. Soon he was back and John handed over uncompleted papers for him to work on. Neither ever mentioned the incident again but Smit toned down his belligerence and John took on most of the personal searches and questioning for himself.

In quiet times he often thought of the men, prisoners, guards and officers, he met each day and how little he really knew about them. Those who appeared toughest may in reality prove to be weak. The calmest, most volatile. The most educated a coward and the humblest ready to save your life. Even the little native cleaning woman who smilingly greeted them as she cleaned their quarters could be a Viet Cong at night with a grenade ready to throw at any one of them.

CHAPTER THIRTEEN

The duties came, after a while, to be rotated among the guards as each was stressful in its own way, between night and day, among the prisoners or in the office. When John had the night shift he could relax during the day and liked to spend time in the common room chatting with Greg and whoever else showed up. Often they would watch a movie, Clint Eastwood being a favorite, and then John could almost forget where he was: almost forget the pervasive putrid smell, the thump of distant bombs and, sometimes not so distant land mine, the zing of mosquitoes, and disgust when he found leeches attached to his skin. They drank Budweiser, the only beer that kept its flavor throughout the heat fluctuations of waiting on the Saigon docks, and joked and scarfed down the cookies Mrs. Davison sent every two weeks with three letters enclosed.

Of as much interest to John were the crumpled newspapers his mother packed around the cookies. While others went for the edibles he was smoothing out newsprint and eagerly reading about local happenings around San Francisco. Lots of rallies against the war, the reasons for which he didn't understand but found hurtful.

And then a headline caught his eye: US DETAINEES FROM VIETNAM'S LBJ PRISON CAUSE LOCAL FEAR. He read on, holding his breath. "Several recent threats of violence have been traced to gang members urged on by prisoners recently sent back from Vietnam and now incarcerated at Fort Leavenworth, Kansas. The targeted victims are innocent family of whoever previously antagonized these returned prisoners while in Vietnam." A shiver ran up John's spine as he remembered the sullen anger built into the faces of the men he had signed out for Leavenworth.

John wrote home regularly, telling his folks of his "safe" desk job and loafing with his buddies, so they probably thought their son was having a luxurious paid vacation. What would they think if he told the truth; that he felt like a prisoner himself in this hell hole, that sometimes he was scared to death that this was his life from now on and home a mirage he would never reach and yet, from the snippets of news his mother unknowingly sent each time, he may not be welcomed if he did return.

Did it ever cool off in this country? Instead it just got hotter and the rats that scurried around the garbage cans behind the kitchen just grew bigger.

As he walked to the mess for lunch he heard a commotion coming from the container where the worst of the prisoners had been housed since the fire. He looked through the fence and the big metal box in the middle of the yard appeared to be rocking. Inhuman screams were coming from inside.

Several guards ran by, unlocked the gate and dashed in, guns drawn.

"What's up?" John yelled as another guard passed him.

"Guy gone crazy with heat in there." The guard flung back over his shoulder. "Probably tryin' to bash his brains out!"

The banging and screaming escalated and John watched as an officer raised something up to the small hole which served as ventilation to the storage unit.

"What the hell..." John muttered to the guard who had joined him to watch.

"Tear gas," the man muttered. "Those poor bastards." Shaking his head he walked on.

John stayed a while longer. The only sound now was the hot breeze whistling through the wire fence.

The guards left the compound and as they locked the gate behind them John asked, "Did you kill them?"

The men laughed. "Hell no, take more than tear gas to kill those bastards. Let 'em cook a while. That lot are headin' back to Leavenworth tomorrow anyway. Let's go, guys, I'm starved."

John stood looking across the empty field. Hard to tell good from bad here sometimes. Days he felt he was living a nightmare. He could understand that prisoner wanting to kill himself, caught between claustrophobia and being roasted alive. Such absolute bloody misery.

"Back to work, Davison, New arrivals waiting to be checked in," barked the passing Sergeant.

Well, he wasn't hungry anyway and he turned back the way he had come. As he entered his office John wondered if he could ever again tell a new parolee that LBJ prison was not as bad as its reputation.

Medics came around to check the enlisted men every few weeks and last time they had drawn blood as well as doing the usual tests. It surprised John to be ordered to the hospital for a suspected hemorrhage but he didn't mind. Any change was welcome, especially if, with a bit of luck, he might get a few days in bed.

He was tired when he got off work and walked over to the hospital not far from the hooch where he slept. His first surprising sight inside the doors was a hillock behind a shield of Plexiglas. Reclining on the slope were four Viet Cong, he could tell that by their tattered uniforms, and each appeared to be a new amputee. One had no arms, just bandaged stumps, another missed one leg, a third no legs and the fourth minus one arm and one leg.

They all stared out with unseeing eyes and at first John thought they were blind but then one looked straight at him and the man's mouth twitched as though asking for something. Did he plead for water? John didn't know and was glad when a nurse called him over to sign in at a desk. He was then taken to a room of mostly occupied cots with clean white sheets, given a cotton robe to put on and told to get into bed. Soon after he had settled, a doctor with a clipboard came in and wrote down answers to questions he asked.

By the end of the questionnaire John was beginning to suspect all kinds of symptoms lurking inside his previously presumed healthy frame and he was glad to finally be left alone to sleep.

They brought him dinner on a tray and he went back to sleep only to be awakened when a soldier was brought in on a gurney and put into the bed next to his. It was dark now but for a small nightlight. The new patient tossed and moaned, calling out as though in the throes of a bad dream. "Fever," the night nurse replied when John asked what was wrong with the guy.

John was in hospital for four wonderful, restful days during which they never found any reason for him to be there. The soldier next to him either died or was moved to another ward; he didn't ask, just relished his vacation, eating, sleeping and flirting with the nurses who seemed happy to flirt back. It was a taste of normalcy in what had become a surrealistic world.

"Okay, Private Davison, you're free to leave."

Words which normally would have been welcome sent a pall of gloom over John as he put on his fatigues and left the cool air of the hospital for the muggy, stinking stockade. Doctors had never found anything wrong with him but then he had never asked, not wanting to disturb his comfortable time out. Now he went straight to his office only to be told the new commander had given orders he was to serve as night guard from six pm to six am in the prison compound, starting immediately.

"Okay," he shrugged and went out and across the road to his hooch. When he entered the common room for a cup of coffee four soldiers sat in chairs seemingly oblivious to the TV on which Saigon Sally was distributing fake news . Something was wrong. It was too quiet. John looked around. What was missing.

It hit him: no monkeys! Usually they were twittering and nattering over bits of fruit, pulling faces at whoever looked at them.

"Where's Toby?" he asked the owner of one whose name he remembered.

"Had to get rid of them. Spread disease the new commander said. Came and took them all away." He spoke looking at his boots.

"Where to? Are they testing them or something?" asked John.

"Probably sell 'em back to the villagers for food. They love monkey brains." The man spoke without emotion and John wondered if everyone became numb to loss after a while in this country. He thought of those small wizened monkey faces, trusting round eyes and human like hands reaching out, expecting only treats and good things from their protectors. Now where were they all? He got up and changed the TV station hoping to arouse complaints that would cover the sadness in him. You're not supposed to mourn monkeys when within a mile American boys as well as Vietnamese villagers, were being slaughtered, but tears filled John's throat for those trusting creatures whose carefree chatter had somehow taken the edge off this miserable place. He stuck an I love Lucy tape into the video cam and they all began to laugh.

CHAPTER FOURTEEN

At six in the evening he began patrolling one of the areas that contained the not so serious offenders. They more or less ignored him and after nine o'clock when they were supposed to be in their bunks it got very quiet; only the sullen thud of mortars persisted like distant thunder. John thought that night would never end and when dawn finally arrived and he trudged out of that yard he didn't know how he was possibly going to survive a future filled with night after night of the same seemingly endless boring tension.

But he had no choice and during the following weeks as he patrolled the aisles between the sleeping men, his nerves were as tight as any guitar string, ready for a surprise attack. The last words said to the guard as he walked through the gate to this detail each night was, "Watch my back," and the other soldier would seriously nod back. Many of these detainees were desperate, on the verge of break downs, thrust into a completely alien environment with no recourse to hope. John was thinking about all this one night and was grateful that at least he could leave at six in the morning and spend time with his comrades outside these walls, not like these poor bastards.

Wham! Deafening thunder of mortar fire. The ground shook. Explosions—one after another. "Cong attack!" someone screamed.

The ground rocked and John watched astounded as the prisoners jumped from their beds to kneel and roll on the floor, sobbing hysterically and praying to their gods for mercy.

The mass hysteria reached inside John and made him angry—angry at the prisoners, the mortar rounds still thundering around them, the whole stupidity of everything and he began to yell. "Prayers won't help you bastards. That's Charlie out there after you. Get off your knees. Stop that useless crap!!"He cursed them and everything else with every curse word he knew and the yelling felt good as though he were vomiting up all his frustration and anger at things he had no power over.

The shelling stopped. Night went back to the crickets and mosquitoes. Morning light seeped in and the smell of gunpowder dissipated.

As he left that compound, six am having finally arrived and the new shift taking over, John, as he had trained himself to do, turned his thoughts and eyes away from the conex box in the yard next door. But today again an unholy row was coming from in there and he stopped.

"Prisoner breakdown," panted a guard running by.

John grasped the wire fence with his fingers and watched the rocking of the container as someone inside flung himself against the walls. John began to shake and the wire fencing he gripped drew blood from his fingers. He let go and ran half sobbing, not bothering to hide his state from those he passed and finally the guard at the main prison gate. Back in his quarters he stripped and stood in the shower for a long, long time trying to wash all the badness away. But of course, it couldn't erase the horror from inside his head.

The war was changing. For a few days the sky was crowded with helicopters, the whirring clatter of their propellers seeming to beat the air into a muggy soup. The men watched as the sky filled with paper pamphlets, fluttering down to spread propaganda to the Vietnamese civilians although, as it was written in their language, John could only guess at what they said. As prisoners in their yards ran to catch them they reminded John of children trying to catch snowflakes and he imagined he heard someone laughing which must have been his mistake as no one ever laughed in here.

Once a week each guard had lunch duty. It was the time when prisoners were massed into larger groups and allowed into the mess hall. Everyone was well aware of, and watchful for, racist attacks among the men, for when they happened they must be quelled immediately lest they get out of hand. John was there the day a white man smuggled in a mass of razor blades tied up and down his arms.

Without warning he viciously attacked and slashed one of the other detainees who had evidently harassed him some time before. The victim was a bloody mess before anyone could stop it. This was a reminder for the guards to always be on alert but as John watched the two prisoners being taken away, one to the hospital, the other probably to solitary hell, he felt something break inside and an emotional numbness take over. From that day, as he patrolled this hellhole filled with men he usually pitied for their hollow eyed misery and expressions of fear or despair, he felt nothing. It was as though all feelings had been crushed and now he could do his job without being ripped apart by other men's anguish

His nights walking among the bunks became routine and as he treated the detainees with respect they treated him the same. He recognized when one became overly withdrawn or sobbing told of a breakdown and got him to the prison psychiatrist as soon as possible.

When he saw a body being taken from the conex box one morning his mind refused to think about how that young American had died and instead he hurried back to his hooch and the group of sixteen soldiers who were now his friends. They had a steak and beer party that night and tried to forget where they were.

Sometimes, despite the heat, those off duty would play a game of football, using a helmet as the ball; or play a prank on each other, such as throwing rocks at the privy when someone was inside.

One day John, seeing a soldier enter one inside the prison walls, picked up a healthy sized rock and flung it at the metal side. Instead of the resounding wham he expected, a shout erupted, the door burst open and the occupant appeared, blood pouring from his head where John's rock had hit having accidently found the small ventilation window near the tin roof.

Before John could do anything an officer appeared and placed him under arrest for causing a 'racial incident'. It was only then that John recognized the victim as Robert, his good friend who happened to be black. He tried to explain to the sergeant that it was only a prank gone wrong but the man, especially suspicious of anything racist since the night of the riots, had John taken to the brig while Rob was rushed away to have his head stitched up.

John sat in the small room near the office where he sometimes worked. It seemed like hours that he alternated between anger, frustration and panic.

Finally the door opened. "You can go," said the older guard. "Black dude went to bat for you. Said it weren't nothin' meant, you're friends."

"Thanks," John muttered as he left.

"Be careful. Real sensitive about anything racist. They'd a wanted to make an example of you but that buck put up a real fight to get you loose. You owe him."

John hurried out of the prison and back to his digs across the road. He was shaking. Every moment in this place was like walking a tight rope over a snake pit. But for his friend fighting for him he could be just another LBJ detainee.

When he entered the common room there was Robert grinning with a big bandage across his forehead.

All John could do was go and give him a big bear hug.

CHAPTER FIFTEEN

"Private Davison, Captain Roberts wants to see you."

John's heart sank. Roberts was the camp commandant and rumor had it several attempts had been made to kill him by his own men. John swiped a rag over his shoes, straightened his fatigues and went quickly into the fortress and to the Captain's office. On the way he tried to remember something he could possibly be reprimanded for. It just seemed you couldn't win whichever way you turned in this crazy, screwed up place.

The Commandant was facing away from him studying a map on the wall.

"Sir? Davison reporting Sir." John saluted the man's back.

"Private Davison. You been messing up again."

"Sir?"

"Which will you take court martial or article 15?"

To hell with them all, John thought, never doubting the unfairness of life in this unholy spot. Let 'em try to prove whatever they think I've done. He stiffened his spine and snapped, "Court martial, Sir!"

The Captain turned slowly toward him with what was almost a smile. "Well done on your promotion to Spec. 4, Davison."

For a moment John stood shocked.

"Dismiss,"

"Yes, Sir. Thank you, Sir," and he left.

The promotion didn't seem to make much difference outwardly but inwardly John was elated. Finally he must have done something right. Just when he had begun to think he wasn't good at anything he had managed to give the correct answer. He wasn't even fighting like he had signed up for and couldn't ever try to explain it to his folks.

Back at the hooch the fresh faced country boy, Josh, met him with a big grin. "Hey, you and me, we got leave tomorrow. Twelve hours in Saigon!"

Getting away from here? John couldn't believe it. But next morning at the first bird chirp of dawn he and Josh were walking along the road, away. Soon a jeep picked them up. The engine was too noisy to talk over so John just enjoyed looking at the other early traffic: beat up old trucks, motorcycles, old and young folks on rusty bicycles and more army vehicles.

On the road's edge lay bombed out wrecks. One was still smoking, US army insignia in plain view. A Viet Cong nighttime ambush. Dead American soldiers, maybe like them, going off on leave, then pfft all over. Josh dug John in the ribs and pointed to the other side where two laughing boys rode a cow with enormous horns.

Entering Saigon they were let off on the side of a wide thoroughfare where they stood, disoriented by the transition from grim LBJ to this bustling modern city. John hadn't expected this wide main street with Palm trees down the middle and lanes filled with noisy, exhaust spewing vehicles. Among the cars were bicycles and scooters, often loaded with everything from whole families to furniture and live chickens. Josh pointed to a bicycle, a huge basket on the front with a man in a business suit reclining in it. Now John noticed many of them weaving through the throng, each with a passenger. 'Pedicabs," shouted Josh grinning. The noise was overwhelming, horns blared on the road and music screeched from a nearby bar. No traffic rules at all by the look of it and John wondered how any pedestrian could ever cross the street. Smelly too, like garbage left out on a hot day; which, he thought, seeing the rotting fruit and vegetables in the gutter, each pile breeding rats and its own swarm of flies, was evidently the case. Something tugged on his sleeve and he looked down into the grinning face of a Vietnamese boy.

"I good guide. I good guide," the kid repeated still tugging his sleeve. "I show you." The child wore a t-shirt and shorts, his brown legs like sticks and his collar bone showing how little meat was on his skeleton. "I good guide," he repeated, brown eyes pleading now.

John looked at Josh who shrugged. 'Okay, you show us Saigon,' he said to the boy.

The sidewalk was as crowded with people as the street was with traffic. Vendors sold drinks from stalls set up outside shops. Some had barstools, some not. John recognized fruit being squeezed into tall glasses and at another makeshift counter beer foamed from suspiciously hazy mugs. Pedestrians were dressed in every type of clothing from the native tunics and conical straw hats, to fashionable western suits and frocks. Many people wore masks against the smog and John, made conscious of the air pollution, felt his eyes sting. Loud music wailed from the open doors of bars but John felt no wish to enter even though pretty Vietnamese girls smiled and beckoned. Now he began to notice the beggars hunkering against the walls, often missing arms and legs, or baring horrible scars. All wore tatters of Vietnamese army uniforms. People seemed to make a point of not seeing them and he wondered if their army just abandoned its men when they were of no use. John was getting depressed and the humidity was getting to him. It must be over one hundred degrees.

He began to notice other things such as bombed out buildings and piles of rubble, remains of the recent Tet offensive. Was it imagination that he felt some people draw away and flash angry looks as they passed?

The boy led them up side streets and stopped in front of an impressive cathedral. Saigon's Notre Dame Basilica a sign said. After that the boy took them to other fine old buildings and John wondered why the signs were all written in French. He was surprised when Josh explained that Vietnam was a French colony. "That's what the war was about originally, these folks want their independence."

All at once John realized how little he knew about this country he thought he had signed up to save from communism. He had just assumed it was filled with small Chinese people like those in San Francisco's Chinatown to which his parents had taken him—as if to a museum or the zoo. He had never thought of Vietnamese as being different; never considered studying their culture... or their history and what they wanted. "So all these fancy buildings were built by the French?"

The kid who had been listening, grimaced and pointed his thumb to the ground, "French, fuck 'em." His small face contorted into a snarl.

"Americans good then?" John said.

The child stared at him for a moment then spun away and motioned for them to resume their trek.

John was longing for one of those fruit drinks he had seen earlier but when he mimed drinking, the kid just led them on, up and down wide streets and narrow. Finally they reached what seemed the dead end of an exceptionally filthy alley.

"I'm not sure I like this," whispered Josh.

"Just a kid," John whispered back but he had read a handout on what to be careful of when visiting Vietnam and special warnings of not to trust anyone.

The boy had stopped and now faced them. "End tour," he said. "You pay now. Fifty US dollah."

"What!" It burst out of both soldiers. "You said fifteen earlier."

The boy's face went hard like a much older man's. "Fifty!"

The alley seemed even darker and John's mind repeated warnings that the most innocent looking might lure the unwary American into a trap. Shivers crawled up the back of his neck as he looked into the hard eyes of the boy who had just spent hours cheerfully leading them.

"Fifty. US dollah," he repeated.

"No," Josh still held out the five dollar bill.

The kid didn't even look at it. Just glared into the faces of the two American soldiers John had been told every native had been taught to hate. One of the child's hands went into his pocket and came out with a whistle.

John automatically went for the 45 he carried strapped hidden under his left armpit.

Without a word the kid took off running. They could hear his sandals slapping echoes against the alley walls. And then just quiet.

"C'mon," John said. 'We gottto get out of here; kid might have friends."

They found they weren't far from bustling areas, now all colorfully lit and even louder. Especially one street which reminded John of a very large flea market. When he looked more closely he saw that the tables were filled with American goods; radios, t-shirts, Adidas, comic books, Coca-Cola. Things usually sold at the army px but in short supply lately.

Seeing their puzzlement a Marine, leafing through some "Look" magazines nearby, leaned close. "All this stuff's stolen when U.S. ships unload at the Hanoi docks. Supposed to be for us troops but…" He shrugged and went back to his 'Look'.

The two returned to the main street, recognizing its wide river of vehicles and following it to where big buildings changed to small and the noise of honkytonks fell behind them. Neither spoke.

John was overwhelmed by all he had seen and heard and smelled. Most of all he felt sad for the skinny child who had led them all day and then run off without any payment at all. They hadn't even bought him anything to eat or drink. Not themselves either but they weren't half starved like that kid.

"You boys want a ride?" A jeep pulled up alongside and they gratefully climbed aboard.

Next morning John sat down to write a letter home to tell of his day in Saigon but it all turned into such a jumble in his head he soon gave up and watched a movie instead. It worried him that he had no handle on his life anymore and, from the bits of news he heard, terrible battles were going on not far from the prison and both American, Vietnamese and Vietcong were being slaughtered in great numbers. Yet here he sat—feeling a prisoner himself. What had all his training been for? Spending every night walking between rows of sleeping men. Bored by the long hours yet startled into terror by the screams of men driven to madness by the heat and attacks by other prisoners.

John just felt numb and helpless and trapped while bombers flew overhead and the thud of their bombs landing: killing humans, no matter who or what nationality, was something he couldn't think about. But in his dreams he smelled gunpowder and charred flesh.

CHAPTER SIXTEEN
Monsoon Season

Rain pounded as though it would never end. The prisoners stood out in it, hunched and miserable, boots leaking, but chose that rather than miss the small bit of freedom they were allowed. "At least it's warm," John told himself as he ran past them from lunch back to his hooch where he drank beer and watched movies most of the afternoon. There wasn't much to talk about with whoever wasn't on patrol at the time. The American radio news was all conflict and whenever there was another big anti-war demonstration back home the prisoners in LBJ became agitated. John then had to anticipate a rough night when all whites stayed well away from any blacks and he had to watch his back every second.

He wrote letters home and found himself borrowing things to write about; such as ambushes of himself and his platoon while hunting down Cong in the jungle when in reality he'd only heard newly arrived prisoners telling about their battles. Some stories he made up entirely. His folks always wrote how proud of him they were and how they expected the war to end any moment now. At the same time papers informed him he would be scorned when he did return. Called a baby killer. John had never felt so deserted and alone.

He was writing one of those letters when the soldier who had taken over his job in the office burst into the room and flung himself wearily down on a chair.

"This damn rain. Hey, Davison, heard news of the unit came over around the same time as you. Got ambushed a couple of days ago. Several killed. One an Eskimo, of all things."

John felt the breath knocked out of him. Not Ben. Couldn't be Ben.

"Never met an Eskimo," the voice kept on but John no longer saw the speaker, all he saw was the round smiling face of his Eskimo buddy as he raised his hand in farewell, and heard his voice saying, "See you in Nam!"

"Didn't get his name did you? Wasn't Ben, was it?" He held his breath afraid of the answer.

"Why, yeah, I do believe it was. Like Big Ben the bear 'swhy I recall it. Bears and Eskimos, y'know. Shit, I gotta get out of these wet clothes."

John hardly noticed the man leave the room all he had in his mind was the smiling face of his friend. Only now it was covered in blood like the man beaten to death on the night of his arrival at LBJ.

Vietnam seemed lonelier now even though he'd barely thought of Ben since coming here.

The nights patrolling the barracks were endless boredom interrupted by the shock of mortars landing nearby, sudden scream of a sleeper's nightmare and thudding rain on the roof. Everyone in this fucking place hated him; he could almost smell the hatred, just because of what he was and the power he had of keeping them in this hellhole. And, of course, the blacks just because he was white

Sometimes he longed for something, anything, to actually happen to break the monotony and uncertainty. With news of ever larger marches and more violent racial unrest back home he could feel the rage stirring in the prison's Black population and feel how it boiled in their veins as they glared when he passed. He kept one hand near the grip of his gun at all times. Now, even while he slept.

Rain was the new normal and everyone was used to always being damp, feet moldering in their boots and the pounding of it making everyone shout to be heard. The pervasive rotting smell of the country blotted out all memory of roses and lilac. That was until the one dismal afternoon when mail delivered a well packed gift to Private Jackson. They all watched as he carefully unwrapped a delicate porcelain cup and saucer decorated with roses and lilac. It was the kind of thing everyone imagined their great aunt having in the parlor back home when lady friends came for tea. However strange it seemed as a gift to send to a soldier in Vietnam Private Jackson had his coffee in it from then on and each time John saw it he was enveloped by a feeling of comfort and promise that there still was a civilized world out there somewhere.

Christmas and New Year's came and went with turkey and cranberry sauce, carols over the loudspeaker and fire crackers at midnight—all feeble attempts at celebration which only made everyone, guards and prisoners, more homesick

Some days were lighter rain that others and on one of these John received permission for a 24 hour pass. In no time he and two buddies were in the back of a jeep hurtling toward Saigon. The rain actually stopped and the road was filled with the usual busy traffic of bicycles, animals and motor vehicles.

"These people don't even seem to know there's a war on," he shouted into the ear next to him.

And it was true. In Saigon streets bustled with shoppers, women and children, country folk with produce to sell, music blaring from the dark interiors of bars. John's mind fought to accept the contrast. Which was reality?

The soldiers he had come with disappeared into a bar but John wandered on, wanting to stay outside now the rain had stopped. He found himself in the street which he had previously thought of as a flea market and paused to hover over the purloined American goods, enjoying their familiarity and lost in the chatter of bargaining.

He rustled through the pages of a fairly recent "Life" magazine and stopped at photos of a girl crouched by the body of a dead fellow college student. "What the…"

"Yeah, I agree."

John hadn't realized he'd exclaimed aloud but now he looked at the man next to him wearing a green jumpsuit with the insignia of a helicopter pilot. "I don't understand what's going on over there!"

"I don't understand what's going on over here. Hi, my name's Jack."

The pilot held out his hand and John took it thinking how good it was to shake hands instead of saluting, and to use first names as he said, "Good to meet you, Jack. I'm John." Maybe there was some normalcy left in the world.

"Darn muggy. Feel like a fruit drink? I've got them from that stall over there and they're good."

They walked over to where a small Vietnamese woman beamed at Jack as if greeting an old friend. Without asking she tossed fruit into a blender with ice and poured the resulting drink into two glasses, putting them in front of the two men who sat at a makeshift table. John had been careful to sit with his back to the wall.

"You and your friend enjoy, Mr. Jack!" The little woman patted the pilot on his shoulder and went to serve another customer.

"Wow, she acted nice. They sure hide it well," said John,

"What d'ya mean? They love us here."

"Where've you been, Man? Vietnamese all hate American's guts. Sweet smiles in the day, doing our cleaning and washing, then at night they get their bazookas and are out to kill us. I've been well warned about them." John took a swig of his drink. It really was good. "You're up in the sky though. It's different down here. Feel someone has his sights on you all the time."

Jack leaned back and stretched his long legs out in front of him shaking his head slowly from side to side as the ice clinked in his glass. "Man, you sure ain't bin where I bin. That's for sure. Where are you stationed anyway?"

"LBJ prison. I'm a guard there."

"Poor bastard. Hear that's a hell hole. Not Vietnam at all."

"No picnic for sure. But we were warned about coming into Saigon. Watch your backs they say. All I do everywhere it seems. American prisoners hate us, natives hate us and folks back home hate us. Sometimes I wonder…"

They were quiet while the little woman refilled their glasses.

"Let me tell you what I did yesterday." The pilot leaned back in his chair, sucked in on his cigarette, squinted and blew smoke upward. "We got word the Cong were heading toward a village where I knew our boys would be waiting for them. Place would be wiped out, villagers slaughtered, caught in the middle. Me and my five crew got there first and you've never seen people gladder to see anyone. Women and children piled aboard the 'copter, then the men who wanted to come. Packed in like sardines they were. When we let them down in a safe place you've never seen folks more grateful. Can't tell me they don't love Americans." Jack stared unseeing ahead of him. "Hell of a thing this dumb war. All they wanted was to get rid of the French… to rule themselves. Just simple farmers in the countryside. Minding their own business. Then the Cong got into it. Infiltrated. Them you do have to look out for." Jack looked quickly at his watch. "I gotto get back to base. Flying tonight." He stood up and held out his hand." Good talkin' to you, John. And believe me, these are good people. Hope we meet again."

John watched him stride away. But they killed my Eskimo buddy, he thought, and stood up leaving a tip for the smiling proprietress. John wandered down the street. No one paid any attention to him.

Music poured out of a bar doorway. Why not go in, maybe a drink would cheer him up. "Hey, watch it, Soldier!" He'd almost been bowled over by three happily inebriated Americans who proceeded to apologize profusely. The smallest of the three stopped in mid-word, staring at John. "Davison? Is that you?"

John stopped breathing. "But you're dead," he whispered.

"Not me!" And the only Eskimo John had ever known sprang forward to wrap his old friend in a crushing hug. After introducing him to his buddies, the four of them swung back into the bar, ordered a round of beers and settled at a rickety table in a corner.

To John it was like a dream, seeing his old sidekick sitting there across from him talking about all the crazy things they'd done in basic. Time and beer flew past until the only light left was artificial.

John had trouble making out the time on his watch and even more trouble standing up. "Gotto get back," he mumbled.

"You stay with us. Camp just outside town. Dangerous going far this time of night."

The four soldiers weaved down the street, supporting each other, laughing, John in the middle. "I gotto learn to hold my likker,' was the last thing he remembered thinking before he felt himself dropped onto an army cot and a blanket thrown over him.

Something happened in the night. Whatever it was it was annoying, as he was having the best sleep in a long time; dreaming his Eskimo buddy was alive. But through the mists of his drunkenness John became aware of people trying to get him up: to shelter him somewhere safe, they shouted. But John knew if he let himself wake up Ben would be dead again and he couldn't bear that. And so he slept on while all hell broke loose and his friends had to run for cover, leaving him to his fate and the Viet Cong.

Brightness hurt his eyes, so he closed them again. From the crow of a rooster John knew it was morning but where on earth was he? As a breeze blew across his face he mentally cussed someone for dumping him in a field overnight.

"Hey, you alive, Man?"

John carefully looked up and saw Ben the Eskimo peering at him. Other soldiers craned past his shoulder as though beholding a miracle.

"What the hell's the matter with you guys? What was I drinking anyway, my head's about to bust open." He squinted at his watch then bolted upright. "I gotto get back to LBJ! What the hell..." he looked from side to side where instead of walls there were huge ragged holes.

"Rockets. Cong attacked in the night. We tried to get you out but you downright refused to budge. Had to leave you. Shell came right through that side of the tent and out the other, right across your sleeping body."

"Man, had you sat up the wrong moment you'd a bin taken out. Miracle it is for sure." The other soldier whose name John couldn't remember still looked slightly in shock and had to be nudged by Ben to help John out of bed. The three helped straighten his clothes so he was at least fairly presentable and as they helped him outside John looked back at the two huge holes on either canvas wall where the shell had torn through while he slept calmly beneath. He remembered his mother's words as she read out loud from newspaper articles reporting horrendous accidents where the victim had survived. "God takes care of drunks and fools," she'd say as though imparting words of wisdom. John had always wondered whether she was advising him to be a drunk or a fool. Now he wondered if she had been making an excuse for her own drinking but it had sure worked for him this time.

"Got you a ride with a buddy heading your way." Ben helped him into the jeep that pulled up in front of them. "Keep your head down now."

"That goes for you too Ben. And no more dyin' ya hear! Bye, Eskimo!"

"Bye, now. See you after the war!"

And the jeep pulled away obliterating sight of John's friend in a spray of mud.

CHAPTER SEVENTEEN

The rain finally stopped for good. Assignments were now spread out, alternating posts among the too few guards, and John was relieved not to have to patrol the barracks every night as had been his lot recently. One or two of the guards were always visiting the camp psychiatrist on the verge of a breakdown. It was the constant awareness that even escorting a prisoner to the latrine or fetching him medication could be the opening for an attack. Other guards broke under the strain but John prided himself on not needing help.

"You got to walk guard for Pritchard tonight, Davison."

The order was like a physical blow. John had expected the night off after guard duty the night before when one prisoner, in his sleep, had kept calling for his mother. That big tough black guy had sounded like a small lost child.

Recalling it now, to his horror, John burst into tears.

The Sergeant waited until he pulled himself together. "What's the matter, Soldier?" he asked in a voice surprisingly gentle.

"I just feel so sorry for them all!" John blurted. For an instant he felt a hand on his shoulder and heard a soft voice say, "It's okay. Soldier." Then he was alone.

Daytime work in the office was like a holiday, being inside with a cup of admittedly bad coffee always near at hand. The days when he strip searched and signed in new arrivals were always stressful though he tried to make it as easy for the poor bastards as he could. Then there came time when the prisoners, shackled and manacled, were taken to Bien Wah airport and sent back to prison in the states. Which was best, the devil they knew or the one they didn't?

A guard had to accompany them on the drive to the plane, a sought after duty just for the chance to get off base, so John and Smit took turns, and this time it was John's.

Dammit, he shouldn't have had so many beers the night before or maybe it was a fever coming on John thought as he entered the office. Smit was already there, glum as usual. "Hey, you want to go 'stead of me, I feel crappy today," John announced.

John would never forget how the private's eyes lit up or his effusive thanks before bolting out the door.

It was a long, boring day and when he went back to his hooch that evening John's spirits lifted to find a package had arrived. He took it down to the common room, set it on the table and opened it to release the aroma of warm kitchens and home. "Help yourselves, boys, Mom's done it again. Chocolate chip."

Nobody moved.

"Come on, Guys. Eat up before the rats get 'em!" John grabbed one and took a delicious bite.

"You haven't heard have you. Mine blew up Smit's jeep on the way to the airport. Everyone dead. Two prisoners, driver and Smit."

"Had three kids and a wife back home too," said someone else

Suddenly John's cookie tasted like poison and he spat it out. I killed him, was his immediate thought. Should have been me with no kids or wife. And the poor bugger envied me my cookies. Should'a bin me…

CHAPTER EIGHTEEN

Of all posts John actually enjoyed being up in one of the guard towers at night. There, ignoring sounds of distant battle, he could look up at the same stars he had known as a child. Just staring into that familiar heaven made LBJ, Vietnam, the demonstrators back in the States and all the misery of this place fade into insignificance.

Then one cloudy night his peace was shattered by the thud-thud-thud of Helicopters. They swooped out of the darkness seemingly straight at him, and gunships thundered close. John's perch trembled and somewhere some one or some thing screamed. Spfft! Spfft! Spfft! Tracer bullets streaked. "Vietcong attacking Long Binh," crackled over the radio. Then static. Now all hell broke loose. A light show of red tracers sliced through fog. Explosions shook every nerve in John's body. His tower shuddered as he watched. Caught up in the beauty and excitement of it all he ran back and forth following the action as Choppers appeared and disappeared like camera flashes. The sounds stirred his soul like a mighty orchestra.

During a moment's pause John wondered how many of the enemy were being ploughed into the ground outside the walls below him. Then he remembered the order that if the Cong ever broke through, weapons must immediately be issued to each prisoner. And who would be the first person they'd shoot? Me, thought John knowing that he, up here in his tower, would be their first target.

Now he had even more at stake in this battle and, adrenalin flowing, he cheered on the helicopters, shouting encouragement, There was only him in this whole war torn world, quivering, every nerve atingle with excitement. Every rocket with him riding on it.

Eventually dawn crawled in sucking away the fog and the helicopters with it.

Nothing stirred. John thought back over the night. It was like a show put on especially for him. Interesting that war could be so beautiful and exciting. Perhaps if he had been sent into the field as he'd expected he would feel better about everything, have excitement and buddies to care about and share things with.

"Hey soldier, you're off duty now." John's replacement appeared at the top of the ladder.

"Many Cong killed?" John asked collecting his belongings.

"Copters did a good job. Infantry out there now prying up bodies mashed into the ground. Heard they found dead with their weapons chained to their wrists." The fresh guard removed his jacket as sun burned off the last of the mist and now brought sweat beading out on both soldiers' brows. "Sometimes ya got to wonder. Right in the middle of it all Col. T. made his driver take him out there. Got plugged right in the forehead pretty well immediately. Driver came back all shook up. We asked why he went out in the first place. He just shrugged and said Col. told him to; wanted to see the show up close. What the hell are we becoming out here?"

John said nothing, just saluted and left.

He went straight to the mess and as he scooped up scrambled eggs he remembered the high he had gotten up there in the guard tower with gunships playing tag among the clouds and tracers flashing color magic. The excitement was amazing—was that why the Col. had gone out to join it? Or was he committing suicide?

John realized he'd not thought once of the pain being inflicted on the ground—but the Viet Cong weren't humans were they—isn't that what he'd been taught in boot camp?

CHAPTER NINETEEN

The months passed, each day marked off on the calendar until his tour of duty would be over. In a way, although eager for the date to arrive he also dreaded it, unable to understand the antiwar demonstrations he imagined personally aimed at him by the people he thought he had joined up to fight for. He now tried to avoid any news from back home but it still seeped through and when he felt more intense agitation among the prisoners he guessed Anti Vietnam riots must have surged in the States.

Every few weeks he got leave and went into Saigon, often now hitching a ride on one of the helicopters he had discovered flew from the nearby heliport. He learned to sit on his metal helmet while in the air to thwart bullets often fired by snipers from the ground. Coming back late at night in a jeep, the helmet would be on his head to protect that most vulnerable part from landmine explosions.

In the city he always hoped to see either his Eskimo buddy or the helicopter pilot, Jack, but he never did, usually ending up in a bar with other G.Is. drinking too much.

Two weeks left. Fourteen more days in this hell hole and he'd be home. Could it really happen? John was suddenly seized with the fear of sudden death in these few days left and conversations and news reports seemed saturated with stories of soldiers being killed during their final days of active duty. These thoughts preyed on John's mind so his stomach became so upset he spent his last days living on Pepto Bismol.

He scarcely ever put down the short timer's stick which proved to everyone, including himself, that it was true, John Davison was going home!

At ten in the morning of November 9th, 1969 John climbed aboard a jeep with a couple of other GIs and was driven out through the gates of LBJ prison for the last time. He did not look back. As they travelled down the road he silently prayed over and over that no mines would be in their path and when they reached Bien Hoa airport and his eyes fixed on the United airlines plane that waited shimmering in the sun he drew in a deep breath and let it out very slowly.

Soon he was aboard, sinking into a soft seat, hearing the hum of the engines and murmur of voices. The stewardess gave the wonderfully familiar instructions in American and he fastened his seatbelt. As the plane took off and gained altitude John looked down at the land which had kept him in a prison for fourteen months. It held nothing he would miss, the smells, the thump of mortars, the heat, the fear. "Goodbye, Vietnam," he murmured and turned to accept the breakfast offered by a smiling American stewardess.

Okinawa. After a brief stop there, the next time he awoke was when the plane was landing at Travis airport. As he looked out at the familiar California landscape tears flooded his throat. Tears of love for his country and the home he had so often doubted he'd ever see again.

The plane taxied to a halt and as they stood on the tarmac after disembarking John noticed they were at the end of a runway far from the airport buildings. He asked a baggage handler why.

"To avoid the protesters, Sir." The man, avoided John's eyes. "They meet every plane with troops aboard. Throw rotten vegetables and stuff, Sir."

John hardly had time to register what the man said before being ushered aboard a bus and driven toward Oakland.

He looked out on all the familiar fields and the freeway crowded with speeding, shiny cars. Then there was Mount Diablo that familiar landmark that meant home. John was glad he hadn't told his parents he was coming, just being here was all he could take right now.

They were let out at the army base in Oakland where they were officially discharged from the US army. It was hard to take in, and John grabbed a cab and had it take him to the Leamington Hotel. There he got a room, ordered room service to send up fried chicken and French fries which tasted better than he ever remembered them, showered and fell into the softest bed he'd lain on for what seemed forever.

CHAPTER TWENTY

Butterflies fought in his stomach. He was almost home. In a few hours he would walk through town resplendent in his dress uniform for all his old acquaintances to admire. The other people in the store where his mother worked would laugh to see how she reacted when he walked in. He wanted his appearance to be a complete surprise.

He shaved extra carefully then showered and dressed, smoothing every trouser crease to perfection. Gave a rub to his shoes, put on his cap then took it off and tucked it under his arm. He looked in the full length mirror and was pleased with what he saw—a good representative of the US forces. Perhaps the local paper would send someone to take photos and write an article.

Too excited to eat John made coffee in his room and waited for ten o'clock to call a taxi.

The driver opened the trunk for John's duffel bag. "Active duty?" he said.

"Vietnam. First day home," replied John.

"Fucking draft." The driver slammed the lid and gestured for John to get in the back seat while he got in front. "My brother got the lottery and bolted up to Canada. I'm lucky—got bad feet. You couldn't find a way to get out of it?"

He pulled into traffic and onto the freeway, too busy weaving in and out for more conversation.

John sat back wondering how anyone could admit to being such a coward as this man had.

Everything looked the same—as if he'd never left. Through the tunnel—and there were the green rolling familiar hills. "Let me out on the edge of town." He would enjoy the walk and probably have plenty of offers to carry his bag. He paid the driver, ignoring his pause for a tip, then slung the duffel over his shoulder and with a joyful heart set off.

It was still early and there were only a few people out yet; those who were seemed not to notice him. It was as if time had stopped for everyone but himself. One child holding his mother's hand squealed, "Look, Mom, a soldier!" John smiled at him but his mother jerked the boy away into the post office doorway. John walked on touched by a cloud of disappointment. Where were all the hand shakes and "Welcome homes"? He walked into the department store where his mother worked. There she was at the far end hanging some clothes on a rack. She looked up and for a moment there was no recognition, then her face lit up and she ran to him, and hugged him. She was crying, "You didn't tell us!"

"I wanted to surprise you." His eyes were wet too.

The store's owner walked by.

"My son, John, back from Vietnam," she said.

The man grunted and walked on.

John's mum looked embarrassed. "People are really against that war," she said to John. "Don't mind, if they seem rude. Go on home and take that uniform off then they'll forget all about it. You didn't kill anyone, did you, John?"

"No, I didn't," he answered truthfully as his mother pushed him out the door.

"I'll be home around five thirty. I'll bring crispy from KFC."

The village was busy now and no one seemed to notice him at all.

When he reached the familiar tree shaded house of his childhood their neighbor was putting out his trash can. "Hi, John." the man said. "Haven't seen you around for a while. Guess your mom told you, Joey got accepted to Harvard. We're pretty proud of that boy, I can tell you." He gave a wave of his hand and trudged back up his driveway.

John watched him for a moment then walked toward the home he'd thought of so often while suffocating in the heat, smells and nightmares of Vietnam. The door was locked and the key wasn't where it used to be hidden so he climbed in a window. His feet had barely touched the floor when a red ball of fur hit his stomach. "Shannon!" John gasped as the dog whirled, lashing her tail and yelping her joy. When things settled down John grabbed an Olympia beer from the fridge, ripped it open, flung himself onto the couch with Shannon beside him, and waited for his dad to come home.

"Good God! Mom told me you were here!"

Dad's booming voice awoke him and he jumped up and into his big bear embrace.

"Hey, how about some chips and another beer." He'd gone into the kitchen. "Gotto tell you about the great day I had. Local grocery stores ordered ten cases of ketchup and..." He sank onto the couch beside John and patted his knee. "Darn good to have you home, son. Mom's been drinking a bit and your sis, she's staying with a friend a few nights, is all excited about being picked for the drill team. Doing right good at school too. Let's see what's on the news today. Big game, ya know... Expect Dodgers 'll win."

Isn't he at all interested in what I've been doing, John thought as the news came up on the old TV. There were people marching, carrying signs. "Murderers." "Baby killers."

"OK if I shower and change? Think I'll go down and see if any of the guys are around."

"Sure, Son," His father barely took his eyes off the game which was starting. The sounds of 'God bless America' followed John out of the room.

He drove his old car down town to the bar he used to hang out at. Several of his school buddies were there and after saying "Hi" continued their conversation of local gossip, the game

John had left his dad watching and the job situation. One of the gang had skipped to Canada to avoid the draft and they discussed the merits of going themselves if their numbers were drawn. No one seemed aware of where John had been recently or cared. They all seemed so callow and ignorant. He had nothing in common with them anymore and he soon left. Tomorrow he and Shannon would go for a long walk and he'd tell her all about it.

As he drove out of town John looked up at the night sky— the same stars and the same moon he had looked at from the guard tower just days before. He had a scary feeling of being alone and belonging nowhere. Who on earth was he?

Without thinking he had driven up into the hills where he pulled into a view point and parked. Below lay the twinkling lights of cars crossing the bridge to San Francisco, serene and beautiful. And so peaceful.

"What does it matter what others think—why should I give a damn if they don't understand. I went when my country asked me and I'm bloody proud I did." John rolled down the window, leaned out and shouted into the clean fresh wind, "You America, were worth every bloody, stinking minute of it!"

With that he started his old Chevy's souped up engine, pressed his foot on the accelerator and with a squeal of tires, roared toward home.

PATRIOT

I was walking the streets of Flagstaff, Arizona. It was Christmas 1967.

It was snowing. Beautiful lights on a windswept night glowed through crystal clear windows, casting a Christmas ambiance over the entire town.

I felt good and secure and comfortable.

That wonderful feeling of youth when you know all things are possible in every way and every new morning is the start of another beautiful day.

I heard an explosion. I awoke with a shock. I was in a foreign land, a war zone called Vietnam.

I had been dreaming I was back in school. The shock of reality went through my brain like a lightening bolt.

I longed to recapture that wonderful dream, but it was too late.

Now it was survival time.

Then I saw the three awful absolutes of war:

Absolute confusion

Absolute terror

Absolute boredom.

I saw friends die and there are still tears of remembrance in my eyes.

I saw the insanity of war, but I did my time. I did not run. I did not hide. But I must confide, I hated every awful moment of it.

Yet in a world of conflict and controversy my feelings are still mixed.

Human nature being what it is will never allow for an easy fix.

Now looking back through all those years and still repressing those stinging tears, I can truly say I've been around life's bend, but for this wonderful country. I'd be willing to do it again.

From the heart of John Robert Davison

BIG RED

I survived the night of the riot
I now thought I had it made
But that awful Big Red
Will go to your head
And you'll find that your life will fade.
The prisoners are looking skyward
Looking for hope so sublime
But the prison's destroyed
And the mind is a mess
Resurrection will indeed take time.

ACKNOWLEDGEMENTS

I want to acknowledge Jil Plummer, a woman who is an accomplished author, a true friend, and a lover of Border Collie dogs. Without her incredible insight and talent this book would not have been possible.

True friends:
John and Kerri Moore, John and Susie Parr, Joanne Davison, Maurine Moody, Tony Mangini, Charles Ingrao, Glen Coons, John Murphy Niemeier, Bill Graham, Bruce Lesser, Chris Flath, Don Rollins, Beth Johnson, Tom Cashion, Gary Hennesey, John Kellogg, Mark Newton, Mike Sugrue, Richard Batchelder, Greg Thompson, Bob Eames, Greg Fehr, Paul Hendrickson

ABOUT THE AUTHOR

Vancouver Island native Jil Plummer has trained horses in England, acted off-Broadway in New York City, worked on a banana plantation in Jamaica, and coordinated a clown show on ABC in Hollywood. While married to a photojournalist she traveled on many assignments throughout the world. She has also taught English as a second language. Jil has published three books (Remember to Remember, Caravan to Armageddon and Amber Dust) and has many more stories to tell.

For more information, please visit: www.jilplummer.com.

CARAVAN TO ARMAGEDDON

The year is 2030. Kendra Savage, 28, a photojournalist, is commissioned to chronicle the journey of thirteen travel trailers, secretly carrying popular celebrities from eleven countries, across the United States.

A great read. Jil has created very fun, complex and creative characters. I loved the book! —Debbie

Travel across the U.S in an Airstream trailer with characters who are not what they seem, including the assassin in their midst. —Dian

AMBER DUST

In this riveting story, which takes us to the Yorkshire moors, the reader is transported to a place rich with intriguing characters and layered with suspense.

I was hooked from the haunting first line. —Grace

The characters, intrigues, and passions in Amber Dust were equal to those I found in the two Pulitzer Prize winners. —Diane

REMEMBER TO REMEMBER

A small child survives the killing Fields of Cambodia.

So inspiring-made me cry. —Ffgffin

Wonderful, captivating and necessary. —D.Yassany